TAMA'GEGA
Fatherless Child

a short novel by

JORDAN DEAN

jdt
Publications

Cover Photograph copyright © Salome Opa

First Edition: December, 2017

The moral right of the author has been asserted.

Published by JDT Publications
Port Moresby, National Capital District, Papua New Guinea
Email: jdtpublications@gmail.com

National Library of Papua New Guinea
Cataloguing-in-Publication entry:

Dean, Jordan. 1984 — .
    Tama'gega – Fatherless Child

    ISBN-13: 978-9980-89-987-3

    1.   A Short Novel by Jordan Dean. 1. Fiction
    PNG/823-dc 22

Printed in USA by CreateSpace Independent Publishing.

COMMENTS BY REVIEWERS

"A superb, gripping and brilliantly written story. The last chapter is a real tear-jerker with a superb ending."

— Chips Mackellar, *Author of Sivarai: Memories of Papua New Guinea*

"A well written novella with an absorbing narrative."

— James Houghton, *Commissioning Editor for Olympia Publishers*

"A simple story, plainly told, of the complexities of family life and love experienced in Papua New Guinea. While the story will have resonance outside Papua New Guinea, the author has imbued it with a local flavour and this is where its attraction lies."

— Phil Fitzpatrick, *Author & Co-founder of Crocodile Literature Prize*

"Jordan Dean's ability to use strong emotional empathy with the protagonist, *Boko*, is through the use of short description and a provocative storyline that awakens one's own remembrances. A promising young writer who demonstrates a deep understanding of managing pain as a craft in his writing. This book is a must read both at primary and secondary school as this is where identity crisis is a real issue at puberty and going forward."

— Loujaya Kouza, *Author, Poet, Singer, Songwriter and former Minister for Community Development*

"An engaging and immersive read. Its evocative and vibrant use of language highlights the distinctive cultural identity of the author."

— Kirsty-Ellen Smillie, *Managing Editor of Austin Macauley Publishers*

"An engaging story with good humour and frank discussions of important issues with good advice. *Sineiyada* reflects the many mothers we know, love and respect. I highly recommend this book to high school students."

— Rashmii A. Bell, *Editor of My Walk to Equality Anthology*

To my two fathers - Dean Magolei and Charles Yobone - for raising me up to be the man I am. I am forever grateful. Thanks for reminding me that there is always good in this world and that there are equal patches of sunshine and rain in life.

To all the children growing up without the presence of their biological fathers, keep hustling and never give up!

Big thanks to Chips Mackellar and Ed Brumby for the comments and editorial assistance. You both are awesome editors.

Sincere thanks to Phil Fitzpatrick for the review and foreword. I am also grateful for the encouraging comments by Loujaya Kouza.

Special thanks to Salome Opa for the beautiful cover photograph.

Jordan Dean

CONTENTS

FOREWORD

Tama'gega is a simple story, plainly told, of the complexities of family life and love experienced in Papua New Guinea. A central theme is the all too common situation where the flux of family dynamics often leads to aberrations in traditional parenting modes.

While the story will have resonance outside Papua New Guinea the author has imbued it with a local flavour and this is where its attraction lies.

It is a short novel, a novella really, but experience tells us that this form suits many Papua New Guinean readers.

Its unembellished text is also an attraction. So often Papua New Guinean writers fall for the lure of excessive verbiage, big words, extravagant detail, unnecessary moralising and convoluted plot. To avoid this easy road takes a degree of skill and discipline. This is not to say there aren't enough twists and turns in the narrative to keep the reader in suspense.

The novel is also interesting because it has equal appeal to both male and female readers. There are strong characters of both sexes and, interestingly, there is no real villain. That must have been a temptation that the author sensibly decided to avoid. In this sense, and particularly where it deals with young professionals, it is a story of the kind that is very relevant to modern Papua New Guinea.

Jordan Dean is an accomplished poet with several books of verse already under his belt. He is also an observant and thoughtful essayist. I hope that this initial venture into the world of long form fiction will not be his last.

Phil Fitzpatrick
Author & Co-founder of Crocodile Literature Prize

PROLOGUE

Sineiyada wiped the sweat on her forehead with a piece of cloth. She bit on her lower lip, attempting to regulate her breath. Fingers clenched tightly, she panted in pain. An old woman, experienced with traditional birthing practices, stood by her side. Her survival instincts had led her to prepare herbs and boil the water for her grandchild to be delivered in case Sineiyada didn't make it to the health centre. She had placed a pandanus mat over the earth and spread a *laplap* on the mat.

Outside the bush hut, a cool breeze came from the ocean. Fireflies glowed in the darkness. The night was broken occasionally by a bat fluttering aimlessly in the sky. Sineiyada was still sweating and panting between waves of pain.

"Push! That's it, keep pushing!"

The night dragged on and the laboring woman's strength was weakening. As a first time mother, Sineiyada didn't know that giving birth took so long. A rusty kerosene lantern, hanging from the sago frond walls flickered, begging for

1

more fuel, before its light was swallowed up by the invading darkness.

The old woman blew on the fire with all her might to get some flames. She then put some special herbs on the fire. The smoke drifted towards the nearby mountains where according to local belief, it would ward off any bad spirits.

Four hours went by. The moon had almost disappeared over the silhouetted mountains. A cry shattered the silence.

A boy was born.

I was born in the early hours of the morning in a tiny village called Iyaupolo on Fergusson Island. Iyaupolo village consisted of seven or eight bush huts made of wood and sago thatched roofing. Near the village stood a small hill called Oya Nainai, which meant 'grass hill' because it was covered with kunai grass.

My village name was Boko. However, my grandparents called me Tama'gega. When I was a little older, my grandmother, Kwasiusiu, told me what it actually meant. Tama'gega means 'father-less' in my native Miapuna language.

My mother, Sineiyada, was only eighteen when she gave birth to me. As soon as I was weaned from breast milk, she left in search for a job and a new life in Alotau. My grandparents showered me with unconditional love and took care of me in the village. I was fed with mashed pumpkin and sweet potato with young coconut juice.

My grandfather, Leidimo, was a warrior, a magician, a hunter, a gardener and a fisherman. I always felt safe with him and I was never hungry. We raised pigs and chickens. At night, we would sit around the fire, listening to grandfather tell stories and legends. I would fall asleep to the lullaby of the nocturnal sounds of the jungle. The hills and jungle were sacred to our ancestors. We respected and worshipped nature. In return, nature blessed us abundantly with fertile soil, yams, taro, banana, fruits, tulip, fish, wood for cooking and building houses. We had everything we needed.

My happy and carefree childhood came to an abrupt end when grandmother passed away. I was five years old at that time. Grandfather did his best to raise me up by himself but since I had to go to school, he sent a message via the health centre VHF radio at Mapamoiwa station for mum to come back for me.

Mum was already expecting a second child. She came back for me when she received the message. Grandfather packed my little bag with the few clothes I had and a lunch box containing cooked sweet potato, taro, tulip and smoked tuna, all crammed together for the long trip to Alotau.

The day when a cargo boat arrived to pick mum and I was probably the most depressing day of my entire life. I remember that day like it happened yesterday. I took one last look at the village. Every single memory of every single experience I've had up to that point flowed through my head like a movie I couldn't turn off.

I burst into tears because I knew those were probably the last happy memories I would have for a long time. I hugged my grandfather, wondering why I had to leave him.

"Goodbye *bubu*," grandfather said in between tears.

And so began my journey in search for truth.

CHAPTER ONE

MY CHILDHOOD IN ALOTAU

Alotau was a sleepy, little town located at the eastern tip of Papua New Guinea. People went about their daily activities at an easy going pace. Life was hassle-free. We lived in a nice, three-bedroom house within the Alotau General Hospital premises at Middle Town. Around our house grew different varieties of flowers. Mum loved flowers and grew roses, daisies, zebras, lilies, orchids, hibiscus, heliconias and desert frangipanis. We even had a cactus growing right in front of the house.

Mum married a man from the Trobriand Islands. To me, he was my father in every sense of the word. His name was Tomwaya but mum usually called him 'Tom'. He was a tradesman carpenter and workshop manager at the hospital. My mum was a beautiful woman with a light brown complexion. She was ten years younger than Tom and docile enough for him to push her around, which he did, all the time.

I had two younger brothers, Willie and Simon. I started school when I was only six years old. Mum enrolled me as Boko Leidimo. Back then, we began school at grade one. There was no such thing as kindergarten or elementary preparatory classes in the education system.

Education was a priority for my mum and I had to excel or face the consequences. The biggest challenge for me was learning to read, write and speak English fluently like the town kids. Otherwise, my childhood in Alotau, for the most part, was pretty normal.

Growing up in a hospital environment, I admired the doctors in their white gowns and my childhood dream was to be a neurosurgeon. I had big dreams and ambitions.

A childhood passion of mine was reading books. I had my own small library. There had been a container of books donated to the hospital and Tom collected several cartons of books for us to read. The floating bookshop, *MV Doulos*, visited Alotau several times. Thus, I had the opportunity to buy as many books as I could afford. Tom built wooden bookshelves in our living room to hold all my books.

School life was a whirlwind. I remembered brimming with joy whenever I received good grades on my report cards. I excelled in primary school. I got the dux award in grade five and second prize in grade six. In grade seven, I came second in Mathematics, first in Commerce and first in Social Sciences. In grade eight, I came first in Mathematics and first again in Commerce.

We had no Xbox or laptops in the early nineties so I would play the 'dictionary' and 'atlas' games with my classmates. There were always new words added to the vocabulary section on the back pages of my exercise books. I knew the capital cities of over a hundred countries by heart. I loved school and learning new things.

One particular memory changed my world. I was fifteen years old, doing grade ten at Cameron Secondary School.

Mum had cooked early that afternoon. She served dinner for us at around five o'clock. We gathered at the table choosing our own side. My little brother, Simon, said he was full when he barely ate a thing. Mum scolded him and told him to eat. We had our dinner in silence.

"Boko, when you've finished your food, we'll go for a walk," mum announced. "Dad and I want to talk to you."

She gazed at me with that distinctive look that she had whenever something was wrong.

"About what?" I asked, worried that I was in trouble.

Tom had just returned home from work, so his clothes had saw dust on them. He stared at me blankly and didn't say a word. I felt uneasy.

Picking up my shoes, I followed mum out of the front door. The evening breeze was cool and the sun was setting over the Owen Stanley Range in the west. We walked down the hill from Middle Town to the beachfront. There wasn't a lot of people on the road that evening. Most people were at home watching the six o'clock news.

We headed for Boss Mei, a small bakery and cafeteria, not far from where we lived. It was usually empty during the week. Mum and Tom were discussing about something in a low tone.

A gentle breeze was blowing from the bay. It made the place cool and I felt sleepy. When we entered Boss Mei bakery, the smell of freshly baked bread, buns and cakes made me hungry again. We sat down at a table in the corner and studied the menu.

"Hello. How can I help you?"

I looked up to see a young lady smiling. Tom asked us what we wanted to have and gave our order to the waiter. I requested for lamington cake slices with orange juice.

When our order arrived, I grabbed my lamington cake slices and juice quickly. As the meal came to an end, mum whispered something and Tom nodded. She cleared her throat and sat up straight.

"Son, we've been hiding this from you since you were born. But it's not fair on your part because you'll eventually find out," she said and paused for a while. "Tom is your step-father. Your real father is someone else."

"What?" I gaped at mum in disbelief.

"Your father's name is Charles and he's from Enga. He's an exploration geologist. Things didn't work out between me and him so we separated. Tom raised you up as his child."

"So..." I started but really had no idea what to say.

To say I was shocked was the least of what I was feeling at that moment. I just stared at mum, then at Tom, searching for answers.

Tom spoke with a guileless expression. "Willie and Simon are still your brothers. I took care of you like my eldest son and they regard you as their big brother. I don't want anything to change."

I really didn't know what I was feeling at that moment. Sure, I was happy to know, but what was wrong with me? I also felt kind of deceived. I wished mum had told me this from the beginning.

Where is my father now? What does he look like? Why didn't he come back for me? Does he even care about me?

I wanted answers to so many questions but couldn't utter a single word. I stared down at the floor for a few minutes trying to digest everything in my mind. The realization that I had a different father was too much for me.

The walk back home was awkward and silent. I barely said a word and my mind was blank. When we arrived home, I quickly marched to my room and locked the door. I just wanted to be alone.

CHAPTER TWO

MY GUARDIAN ANGEL

The next morning, I woke up not sure if I was in the right place. I felt like a total stranger in the house. So many things kept running in my head, more questions that needed answers. I wondered what tomorrow had in store for me. Will I complete my education? Will life be normal like it used to be?

My mind was still troubled. I had to talk to someone who would lend me an ear. Someone who would tell me that everything will be fine and that I would still achieve my dreams.

Knowing the truth about my biological father opened up a new world that frightened and intrigued me. Some missing pieces were put together. I understood more about myself, about my personality and appearance. However, it was like a jigsaw puzzle. A lot of pieces were still missing. Mum was the only one who could put together some of the missing pieces.

After school, I went straight home and took a nap without any thought of food. I woke up later at around four o'clock in the afternoon.

Tom was not home yet and my two brothers were out playing with our neighbor's kids. I resolved to talk to mum. She was watering her flower garden at the back of the house.

"Mum?" I interrupted her.

She looked up at me. "Yes, son. You don't look happy."

"I still don't understand. So my father is different?"

She turned off the hose. "Let's go back to the house, son. I'll tell you everything about your father. I also have something to show you."

I followed mum back to the house. Mum spread a mat and we sat down on the veranda. She began telling me about her life and how it happened. She talked for almost an hour.

Mum told me about her school days. When she was about my age, she loved reading too. Mum was the third born in a family of five. Her parents were simple village people. In the seventy's and eighty's, only a handful of men had formal jobs. The majority of the local men worked as casual laborers for the white men.

Because of the hardships at home, she struggled with her school work. Times were hard but she understood. She had dreams, big and very beautiful dreams. She attended the community school at Mapamoiwa station. She had one meal a day and no school uniform but she endured.

One of her maternal uncles was against the idea of mum been educated. He advised grandfather not to waste his time and throw money to the dogs. But grandfather was a wise man and believed in her. Mum held onto her dreams. She always believed in the beauty of her dreams and wanted to have it. She wanted a better life for her parents and family. She wanted a better future for herself.

Grandfather produced copra to support her but he had four other children to take care of and that was why he couldn't send her to Wesley High School even though she was selected. He had done his best and wanted mum to know that he wanted the best for her. Grandmother sold vegetables and fish at the market to support mum as much as she could.

Because of that, mum came to Alotau where she stayed with her big brother, John, to continue her education at a vocational school.

Some years later, she was employed at the exploration camp site as a laundry assistant and that's how she met my father, Charles. After some messing around, mum was pregnant with me. But her brothers and parents didn't like my father and chased him away. They have heard stories of highlands men marrying many wives and didn't fancy the idea of my mum been in a polygamous marriage.

Mum was heartbroken and was inclined to get rid of me but grandmother scolded her not to do anything stupid. And so I was born a little premature and underweight because mum was depressed about her life. She had not eaten well and had always been crying. Anyway, that was how I came into existence.

Mum went into the house and returned with a photograph of my father. She'd hidden it carefully in her suitcase all these years.

She handed the old photo over to me. "That's your father when he was in America for studies."

I studied it for a while and smiled. He was standing next to a tall building somewhere in America. He had an unshaved beard and wore flair jeans and a shirt which was fashionable at their time, I supposed. I somehow resembled him, I realized.

I was amused. "Does he ever shave?"

Mum's face lightened up a little. "Oh, no. Your father doesn't shave his beard. He told me that it's their culture. They grow their beard to show that they are men and not boys. I used to tell him that he looked ugly with the beard."

"So mum, why didn't you search for my father instead of marrying Tom?"

"Boko! Can you stop asking me unnecessary questions?"

"I need to know, mum!"

"Look son. I am your mother! The one who carried you for nine months inside my stomach, brought you to town, put clothes on your back, sent you to government schools to be educated. I did what I thought would give you the best of everything".

I cringed. "I know but you hid the truth from me for fifteen years!" For a few moments, she stared coldly at me. I probably struck a few cords and mum was clearly pissed with me.

"You are so ungrateful. I should have left you in the village with your grandfather so you can learn how to make garden, go hunting and fishing and be a complete bush *kanaka*," she hissed.

When mum came to Alotau, she lived with her cousin sister, Bona and her husband Clark. Clark was the hospital gardener and they lived in the hospital area too. Tom was a divorcee with two children from a previous marriage. He noticed mum immediately since she was a young, good looking woman. He confided with Bona that he was interested in mum. Bona kept insisting for mum to date him.

Tom would shop and visit them every week just to meet up with mum. After some time, Tom confessed to mum that he wanted to marry her. He seemed to really love my mum, and vice versa. Mum accepted his proposal and moved in with him.

Shortly after they were married, my mother fell pregnant and gave birth to Willie followed by Simon two years later.

"Besides, your father married a second wife straight after you were born. What was I supposed to do? Cry over him and remain single for the rest of my life? I came to Alotau to start a new life. Tom is a good man. He brought you up thus far son."

I stared at mum expressionless. She was a strong woman. To me, she was the epitome of a Papua New Guinean woman, yet at the same time, she wasn't. She was a woman for her family. She believed in her traditions but ruled with an iron fist. I could tell mum was bitter about her past life and marriage. She harbored so many bitter memories in her, memories that she wished she could forget but which she had been forced to accept.

Indeed, some things never disappear from our minds. They only hide somewhere to rest and reappear when triggered.

Mum was truly my guardian angel. I couldn't ask for more.

CHAPTER THREE

MAKING ENDS MEET

Tom lost his job unexpectedly. A jealous work mate had written a fabricated report to the hospital management and he was terminated. Tom sunk into a deep depression, seeking solace in alcohol. It devastated him because he had served the hospital faithfully for more than fifteen years.

Although physically and mentally drained, mum was a wise woman. She managed with whatever little money that was available to keep our family happy. Mum was only educated up to vocational school level but was good with sewing clothes. She would sew beautiful *meri blouses* which she sold for twenty five kina each. She also sewed quilts, bed covers, table clothes and even sewed seat covers for buses to make ends meet.

When she first married Tom, she depended on him for financial support and her wellbeing. She didn't earn much from selling the *meri blouses* and Tom had to provide for most of the things in the house. Tom would complain about his money often.

It was a timely blessing when mum commenced work with Alotau General Hospital as a casual seamstress. She was now the breadwinner, providing normality and stability for the family. Tom started doing odd jobs around the place to support her whenever he made some money from his clients. We lived a simple life.

I went to school without lunch or pocket money. While my classmates with money bought doughnuts or sandwiches and canned drinks for lunch, I would stay hungry the whole day. At times, I would husk dry coconuts behind the boys' dormitory and eat the meat to satisfy my hunger.

It was going towards the end of term four, and notices were given to students with outstanding school fees to complete their payments. I was given a notice to pay up the six hundred kina that was outstanding.

"Please remind your parents to complete your fees or you won't be allowed to sit for your grade ten examinations," Mr. Samuel, our class patron said.

Once or twice, I had given my school fee receipts to the school bursar but they were part payments. Mr. Samuel had to send us back home to remind our parents that nothing was free. There was always a price tag on everything and the school needed money for its projects and many other things.

When the other students left, I sat on my desk thinking about where to find the money to complete my school fees. I hoped that Mr. Samuel would at least be considerate enough so I decided to talk to him.

"Excuse me Mister Samuel." My voice trembled. "Can I talk to you about my school fees?"

"Please talk to the principal. I can't assist you."

I was expecting that answer. Mr. Allan Jones, the school principal was an old, Australian man who had taught in various high schools throughout Papua New Guinea for over twenty years. I decided against the idea of been in the principal's office with a shaky voice, trying to explain my situation.

Besides, I was terrified of white people. I remembered my grandfather telling me that when our people died, their spirits came back in the form of white men. What if Mr. Jones was one of my ancestors? I froze at the thought.

On the way home, I thought of other options to pay my school fees. If mum couldn't afford it, I could collect empty beer bottles to sell. Or perhaps, I could collect empty cans to sell to the recycling company.

Tom was busy working on a wooden trunk box for one of his clients when I got home.

"Dad, I was sent home because of outstanding school fees," I said, showing him the letter.

"Give the letter to your mother when she comes home." He continued with his work without even looking up.

"Okay. Just letting you know." I wanted to throw the letter in his face but I never showed that I was irritated.

When I gave the letter to mum that evening, she went to the room to discuss it with Tom. Some minutes later, I heard them arguing over my outstanding school fees.

"I won't waste my time and money on him!" Tom yelled.

"He is still your son, Tom. In future, you're going to run to him for money."

"I won't bother him. I have my own sons to run to!"

"Fine! I'll get a loan and sort it out but you have to pack and leave! You're living under my roof!" I heard mum shout back and the front door slammed.

I kept quiet in my room. The row had lasted for almost an hour and was just the latest in many since mum started work. I tried to study my notes for a test but couldn't concentrate because of the upheaval.

I heard footsteps along the pathway and peeped out of the window. Mum marched off down the street, her head held high but I knew she was hurting inside. She had told Tom countless times that she wanted to be on her own, but couldn't find the guts to walk out.

It pained me so much. I wanted to return to the village but mum told me to stay and be obedient to Tom. She believed that time would change Tom to become a good man. In fact, mum remained married to Tom because of us, her children. Only time would tell and I just had to hang in there.

I went back to bed and tried to forget about it. I was too young to understand life.

CHAPTER FOUR

LETTERS TO MY FATHER

One afternoon, mum was all smiles when she came home from work. She handed me a small, yellow envelope. It was addressed to me. There was no return address. However, it was stamped by the Post Office in Lae, Morobe Province.

Curious, I turned the envelope several times. "Who is it from?"

"I think it's from your father. We don't have any relatives living in Lae," mum said.

That night, I read through the letter. It was from my father, Charles. He explained why things didn't work out between him and mum and asked for my understanding. He said that I have another three brothers and two sisters in Lae. He also hoped to meet me soon.

I checked my wrist watch. It was a half past eight. The night was still young. I still had an hour and a half before bed time.

Luckily, there was a return address in the letter. I decided to reply Charles letter. I started scribbling on a writing pad.

Dear dad,

Warm greetings to you with the hope that you are in a good health. As for me, I am doing okay I guess.

I am in grade eleven now at Cameron Secondary School. My childhood dream was to be a doctor but my grades in the Sciences were not too good so I am majoring in Social Sciences. I am taking Economics, Geography, Physics, Language and Literature and Minor Mathematics.

Hope I do well so I can get into law school or business school. In the meantime, I am studying hard.

I'd like to meet you and my other siblings there in Lae someday too. Pass my love to them.

Oh and dad, I have one request. Please shave your beard. You'll look nice without it.

Yours truly,

Boko.

I sighed. It was already ten. I went through it one, twice, three times and wondered where I had found the courage to write such a request to my father. I truly feared him. Putting the letter in an envelope, I resolved to post it the following day and switched off the light. It was time to rest.

A few months later, mum gave me another envelope. Charles had replied to my first letter. My heart started racing in my chest. I'd been eagerly awaiting his reply every day. I smiled with excitement as I opened the envelope.

Inside was a photograph of all my half brothers and sisters in Lae. In his letter, he said that he had never shaved in his life. He only trimmed it with a hair trimmer to keep it short. He also said that he wanted me to go over to Lae and attend an international school there. He would arrange with mum for my transfer certificate.

Unable to contain my excitement, I informed mum about what Charles had written in the letter. She was furious.

"What? Is your father out of his mind?"

Mum snatched the letter from me and tore it up. I was terrified and didn't know what to say. She walked over to the side of my bed and sat on the edge.

"Your father abandoned you from birth and never spent a kina on you. You grew up in Tom's house. What is he trying to prove now?" She scorned.

She then observed me with a look of disappointment on her face. "You have a father and mother here and we have good schools in Alotau. You're not going to Lae. Period!" mum stated coldly. "Do you understand me?"

The tone in her voice that was once sympathetic became serious. I may have struck another nerve but I was extremely agitated to worry about mum's emotions.

I nodded. "Yes mum. I am sorry."

She gave an approving look and I could tell she was mentally patting herself on the back for a job well done.

"Tell Charles what I said when you write a letter to him." She stood up and left the room. I sat on the bed, feeling like a beaten puppy. There was so much that my father had missed out on in my life. It was not until recently that he decided to get in touch with me.

That night after dinner, I decided to write another letter to my father to ease my mind. I headed back to my room and switched on the light. There was a lot I needed to get off my chest.

I pulled out a pen and a writing pad. Where to start? I thought for a while and then began scribbling.

Dear dad,

For many years, I never knew about you until lately. You left me at birth and never cared to turn back. There is so much you've missed and I have a lot to tell you.

Dad, I write to you so that you may share my world and maybe give you a picture of the world that you left behind.

I am sure you have learnt to live without me around you. For me, your son, I am still trying to come to terms with everything. Everything seems confusing and I have so many questions but not enough answers.

I would like to go straight to some of the questions that have bothered me but I'll just ask you one for now. You knew mum was pregnant, why didn't you come back for me? You could have at least tried to take me with you to Lae.

Maybe it would have saved me from all the pain and trouble of been mistreated and neglected. Sometimes, I even question my existence. How did I get to be like this? Was I brought into this world to go through such challenges?

Mum won't allow me to come over to Lae. I wished I had a complete family. A father and a mother and not this bullshit of having a step-father.

I'll be graduating next year and I hope I make it to university. I've come a long way without you and I will make it with or without you.

I've ranted enough for now. Thanks for hearing me out.

Yours truly,

Boko.

I put down the pen, leaned back on the chair and rubbed my forehead. I've been wanting to get that off my chest for a long time.

It was still hard to forgive him for deserting me, but deep down, I longed to meet him.

CHAPTER FIVE

BASTARD CHILD

Tom turned out to be very abusive. He started coming home late and argued a lot over little things. One night, he came back home drunk, as usual. He didn't have his dinner even though mum brought the food to him.

"You don't like the food? Have you eaten elsewhere?"

"Damn it, why do you ask so many stupid questions? Don't force me to eat your food when I don't want to!" Tom roared at mum. "In fact, take this crappy food away from me."

"Why are you doing this, Tom?" mum pleaded.

"You should just marry Charles and take your bastard child with you!"

"How dare you say that, Tom? Boko didn't come out from a cave. He has a father and we were only discussing about his education." Mum was now fuming.

Tom slammed his fist on the table. "Shut up!"

I watched helplessly when he grabbed mum by the neck and flung her to the floor. He kicked her in the stomach. Mum cried out in pain.

"I will kill you! You useless woman!" He kicked her again.

"Kill me now! I am tired of living. I am tired of this life. Let me die. Go ahead… kill me," mum cried.

Seeing mum's nose bleeding and lying on the floor in agony made me drop tears. I couldn't fight Tom. I blamed myself as the cause of all the arguments and fights between mum and Tom.

I locked my bedroom door and wished I never existed. I wanted to run away. But how? I wondered. Where do I go?

Tom was a caring father until the day Charles came into the picture. That was when Tom began loathing me like I was a pest that had to be eliminated.

He didn't hit me. He just pretended to be nice when mum was around. When she was not around, he excluded me and made me feel unwanted like I didn't belong there. He would buy my brothers chocolate muffins or ice cream while I had nothing. I was just a child and those actions hurt like hell.

I never questioned why or how different I was to my brothers in appearance, personality or intellect. To me, they were my blood brothers.

As I grew older, he would say sarcastic things like, "I didn't expect to see you here. Thought you'd be out with your friends. Oh, I forgot, you don't have any friends."

I wasn't really a quiet type but just kept my circle of friends small. I was more level headed and preferred to spend time with my books rather than hanging out with dumb friends over the weekends and flirting with girls. I wanted to score straight A's in all my school subjects. In those dreadful days of high school, I consoled myself that getting good grades would land me a high paying job in the future.

Tom hated me even though I was in general, an obedient sixteen year old and by no means a spoilt child. He would accuse my mother of spoiling me when she tried to defend me. Tom became pretty violent towards my mother with his rants and accusations. To keep the peace, I did everything I possibly could to please Tom. I didn't want to see my mother hurt or in tears.

But Tom was never pleased. He did everything within his power to stop mum and me from communicating with Charles. I couldn't fight Tom and mum was too submissive to stand up to him, so he succeeded. I stopped writing letters to my father.

Mum also refrained from speaking to Charles. I never heard from him again. I would take out his photograph from time to time and prayed to meet him some day.

My life became increasingly miserable. All my hopes of meeting my father turned bleak. My future was uncertain and feelings of hopelessness overwhelmed me.

To get rid of all the negative thoughts and emotional turmoil, I'd bury myself in my textbooks. School was the only place that I found some peace.

CHAPTER SIX

ONE CHAPTER CLOSES

The examinations were over. I couldn't believe how time slipped by so fast. It seemed just like yesterday when I arrived from the village and started school, and now I was graduating with a Higher School Certificate.

The graduation ceremony was to be held, as per tradition, at the William Strang Hall. The building was recently renovated and looked new with its decorated walls, ceramic tiled floor and air-conditioning. It was named after one of the pioneer headmasters of Cameron High School as it was known when established in the sixties. The hall had held countless graduation ceremonies and examinations over its thirty year existence.

At ten o'clock, all of us graduating students gathered outside the hall. Everyone looked so elegant. I dressed up neatly in a dark blue suit and expensive new shoes. The shoes felt awkward to walk in but that was a small price to pay for looking sharp.

I followed a long queue towards the large, heavy looking doors which marked the main entrance. The noise of the gathering crowd grew louder as we entered the hall. The hall could seat up to six hundred people however, it was packed with family and friends of the graduating students. Mum, Willie and Simon attended my graduation.

A loud round of applause marked the entrance of the principal followed closely by the staff. That was followed by boring speeches by the board chairman and other dignitaries

I waited eagerly and somewhat anxiously, as I watched my fellow students called up, in alphabetical order, to receive their graduation certificates. Student after student walked up accompanied by a round of applause to collect their sealed certificates representing their hard work and final indication of success.

I must have been in a day dream when I realized that my name was mentioned a second time, rather loudly, by the Master of Ceremonies. I took a deep breath and walked up to the podium.

"Congratulations Boko," Mr. Jones said when handing over my certificate.

"Thank you sir." I shook his hand firmly.

"Keep your head high young man."

This was the day that my twelve years of determination and perseverance in school had led to. It was a significant achievement for me since I was the first person from Iyaupolo village to complete grade twelve education!

I stood with the principal for a few minutes to allow my camera man, Willie and several of my class mates to take photographs. Obviously, I gave my best smile for the cameras.

I had endured all the hardships to get to this stage. I had withstood the challenges of childhood. I was proud and I knew mum and my little brothers were proud of me too. I did it for my family.

After the presentation of the certificates and awards, we made a long queue outside the hall to allow family and friends to shake our hands. I sneaked a glance at my girlfriend Helen. She responded with a questioning gaze.

"Can I have a photograph of us together?" I asked.

"Sure sweet heart, I'd love that."

Helen was my first serious relationship. I never really understood why she liked me. I had a crush on her since grade eleven but didn't have the guts to tell her in person. She majored in sciences so was in another class. I thought she was the prettiest girl in the school. I would gawk at her whenever she passed by our classroom and one of my class girls and a good sister-friend set us up. Helen thought it was cute that I was her diehard fan.

I was nervous at first but eventually got comfortable hanging out with Helen. She was beautiful, had a great personality and was smart. I considered myself the luckiest guy to be with her. I hoped that one day I would marry her and spend the rest of my life with her.

It was a sad moment for us. Most of the students were in tears when the song '*Graduation*' from Vitamin C came on.

> "*As we go on, we'll remember all the times we had together*
> *And as our lives change, come whatever.*
> *We will still be friends forever...*
> *Will we think about tomorrow like we think about now?*
> *Can we survive it out there?*

Can we make it somehow?
I guess I thought this would never end
And suddenly, it's like we're women and men
Will the past be a shadow that will follow us around?
Will these memories fade when I leave this town?
I keep, keep thinking that it's not goodbye
Keep on thinking it's time to fly…"

The lyrics were deep and a few tears rolled down my checks too. One chapter of my life was about to be closed.

That was the last time I saw Helen.

ɀ

CHAPTER SEVEN

CHASING DREAMS

I spent the festive season at the village helping my uncle, Manoa, to harvest sea cucumbers. Uncle Manoa was my mother's last born brother. Sea cucumbers were abundant in the reefs surrounding our village. We would go out diving every day and return with our canoes filled with those slimy, funny looking sea creatures. Sea cucumbers provided a good source of income for the village people.

But, it was a grueling job. Once caught, the sea cucumbers had to be gutted, cleaned, boiled, smoked and dried. I had to collect firewood every day to smoke the sea cucumbers. We filled two large bags of the dried beech-de-mer to sell in Alotau. Uncle Manoa offered to help mum with my school fees if I was selected to university.

Iyaupolo, my native village, is on the west coast of Fergusson Island. It is blessed with the greenery of coconut palms, white sandy beaches, crystal clear sea, cascading waterfalls and tropical rainforests. Going back home for Christmas holidays was something I always looked forward to with much excitement.

Iyaupolo village was devoid of electricity, water supply, basic health and education services. My uncles would walk a fair distance, daily, for a few buckets of water for daily usage. The nearest health centre and primary school at Mapamoiwa station was a two hour walk or paddle away. Education was the key to developing any community, but my cousins' hardly made it past grade eight because of the distance.

Life was difficult. Time had stood still for my insignificant village, unknown to the outside world because it hadn't produced any lawyer, doctor, politician, or influential figure. It was completely isolated from modernity and the rat race of money, power and prestige. Nonetheless, I always enjoyed my time in the village.

This was the life that I once was so reluctant to leave, the life I would have given up anything to return to. Iyaupolo would always have a special place in my heart. It was my birthplace and home.

I remembered when I was a little boy growing up in the village. Grandfather would take me into the jungle with him to go hunting. I would carry grandfather's basket over my thin shoulders to collect the tulip that grew in the wild.

Grandfather would kill any wild pig, bandicoot or wallaby that was unfortunate enough to cross his path. One thing I learnt about grandfather at a young age was that whenever he went out hunting, he didn't return empty handed.

One night, grandmother and I had waited up for him to return from a hunting trip until midnight. We sat on the

31

platform together, watching the track that led up to the river and the mountains. A silhouette appeared and we knew it was grandfather. He walked towards the lantern that we had lit and threw down the corpse of a small pig to reveal the result of his hunting trip.

"That's it?" grandmother asked in a frustrated tone. "You spend the entire day hunting and that's all you bring home?"

"At least we have some pork meat to cook with our yams," grandfather said and sat down to roll his tobacco.

Grandfather had shown me things that were sacred to my people. He taught me spells, incantations, herbs, leaves and roots which were of sacred knowledge that I was forbidden to tell anyone. He washed me with special leaves for protection from bad spirits.

Now, I saw it as the life my mother had heroically rescued me from. The harsh village life had made grandfather age quickly.

The New Year brought with it some hope and optimism. I was prepared to embrace new challenges. Usually, most of the universities and colleges published their acceptance lists in the daily newspapers around late January so mum bought the papers every day to check for my name. I was anxious too.

"Which university did you apply to on your School Leaver Form? And which course?" Mum asked me probably for the hundredth time.

Huh? Which university did I apply to? I hated that question. I hated it so much.

"Bachelor in Business Accounting at the University of Papua New Guinea," I murmured.

I was afraid that my name would not be on the University of Papua New Guinea acceptance list. I somehow doubted myself although I was actually one of the top students.

Finally, the acceptance list came out in the Post Courier and the National newspapers. My name appeared on the University of Papua New Guinea acceptance list for the Bachelor in Business major in accounting course.

I could not believe that I was selected for the University of Papua New Guinea, the premier university in the country. All my uncles and aunties including grandfather in the village got the news that I was going to university.

I didn't know how to express myself. Happiness? Pain? I wasn't sure. Happiness for my performance. I had done well in school and made my family proud. A lot of my school mates were not selected. I had the brains.

I did it for my mother, for my brothers, for my grandfather, for my late grandmother, for my step-father, Tom and maybe for my father, Charles, who I may never meet.

Yet, I was also angry. Maybe it wasn't hatred but bitterness for the times gone and the pains borne. Pain in my heart for all the tearful moments in my life. Pain for my father, Charles, not been around. Pain for been labelled a bastard child.

Of all the people I had worked hard for, Charles was the least. I felt better that way. I saw it better that way. I hadn't worked hard to make him happy or be proud of me. What was I to him, anyway?

I didn't consider him a good enough father to deserve my hard work. If he wasn't around for me since the day I was born, why should I work hard to make him proud? Definitely, not Charles!

Only one person in my life guided me forward when I thought that it was all over. Only one person was there to cheer me up when I was at the point of giving up. That was my mum, Sineiyada.

It was mum that was supposed to feel proud, to be happy and to wear a smile for that success was hers. At least, that was the best gift that I thought I could give to mum in return for the many tears she had shed for me and the battles she fought for me. It was the best I could afford for her.

A tear dropped and I smiled. I wiped it but another one followed, yet another, and another. The smile died as mum hugged me. At least, someone understood what I was feeling.

"I am so proud of you my son," she said.

Mum showed the newspaper to Tom when he came home that evening. He didn't smile or shake my hand.

"Congratulations Boko," he said plainly.

I knew he was pleased with himself because everyone in our Middle Town neighborhood was congratulating him and saying Tom's son was going to university.

When I received my acceptance letter from the University of Papua New Guinea, it stated that I was under a scholarship from the Office of Higher Education. That meant that my airfares and some portion of my tuition fees were paid by the government.

Uncle Manoa sold the beech-de-mer and assisted mum to pay for the student component of my tuition fees and ensured that I had everything I needed for school.

To me, university was the gateway for all my dreams of a better life. As the day crept closer, my anticipation grew.

CHAPTER EIGHT

LAST DAYS IN ALOTAU

I met up with my best friend, Nimrod, from secondary school in town when I went to pick up my ticket from the Air Niugini office. He waved and walked over to chat with me. "Hey dude! Congratulations. I saw your name on the University of Papua New Guinea list."

"Thanks bro. And you? Did you get an offer?"

"Unitech bro! No let down. I am going to the University of Technology," he said with a big grin.

"Well, congratulations bro. I am so proud of you."

I gave him a high-five. Nimrod was in a happy-go-lucky mood and wanted to celebrate our achievements.

"We should have a few cold drinks. I have some money."

"Sounds like a good idea. Our last drink up until we catch up again," I said.

I thought we deserved a drink. Why not? We had done well in school and that was definitely something worth celebrating.

We took a leisurely stroll over to the Garden Bar at Alotau International Hotel. It had the best outdoor bar in town with a million dollar view of the picturesque Milne Bay. Not much was happening that afternoon. The bar was empty.

We sat on the empty stools beside the bar enjoying the cool breeze that was blowing from the sea. Nimrod ordered a stubby and gave the cashier a hundred kina note. "Boko, what will you have?"

"Looks like someone's loaded. I'll have Niugini Ice beer."

"Can or bottle?" the bartender asked.

"Bottle please," I said.

The bartender opened a cold Niugini Ice beer bottle and placed it in front of me. I liked the taste of Niugini Ice. Stubby was slightly bitter to me. I threw up once or twice before. When cold, it tasted good but when hot, it was really bitter. I didn't know why Nimrod loved it. We tossed our bottles and I took a gulp of my beer.

"Aah, nice and cold," I said approvingly.

"Say you graduate with your accounting degree and become a millionaire. What will you do?" Nimrod asked.

Nimrod loved debating about politics, history, current affairs and discussing random ideas in school. He was quite an intelligent bloke but sometimes annoying too.

"I want to travel, see the world. Live like there's no tomorrow. I'd love to see places that I've always dreamt of like Paris, London, Kuala Lumpur or Bucharest," I answered wishfully.

"Bucharest? Where's that?"

"That's the capital city of Romania."

I was quite good in geography class and I loved watching Discovery and National Geographic channels.

"That's cool bro. If I was a millionaire, I'll marry seven wives. One lady for each day!" he said, grinning.

"Damn! I'll marry more than seven," I added and we burst out laughing. "But seriously, I'd love to set up my own business so I don't have to work for anyone. I'll be my own boss."

"That's awesome. I'd like to have a mansion somewhere out of town in the countryside."

I downed my first beer in a few minutes and ordered another one. Nimrod did the same. We were on our fourth bottles when another friend from school, Maela, joined us. He had a gloomy look on his face.

"Hey Maela, what's up dude?" I greeted him.

"Cheers bro. Have one on me," Nimrod said, offering him a drink.

"Thanks brothers," Maela said and sat down on a stool.

"So, what's with the gloomy face?" Nimrod asked. "You didn't make it to college?"

Maela stared dolefully at his stubby. "No, not really. I am going to Port Moresby Business College but…umm, Mele is pregnant."

I frowned and stuck my head forward. "What the heck!"

Mele was Maela's girlfriend since we were in grade nine at Cameron Secondary School. I remembered Maela taking her out for some weekends.

"You should have used a bloody condom! But anyways, congratulations bro. You're going to be a father. You should be damn proud," Nimrod teased, patting Maela on the shoulder.

I couldn't stop laughing at Nimrod's dry sense of humor. He was a clown sometimes.

"Thanks for making me laugh asshole," Maela retorted.

It sounded as if he had just signed his own death warrant and with one long gulp, Maela emptied his beer.

"This calls for a celebration," I quipped.

We ordered three more bottles and we toasted to the soon to be father. Both boys had dated their fair share of girls during our high school days. For Nimrod, he began dating in the ninth grade, and he hadn't gone more than two weeks at a time without a girlfriend since then.

"Guys, the next round is on me," Maela said, still looking depressed.

"So, are you going to continue studies or find a part time job since you're going to be a father soon?" I asked.

"I don't know bro. My parents want me to continue but I don't know about Mele's parents."

"Sorry Maela," I said sympathetically.

We gulped our drinks in silence for a while. Maela should have known better that it wasn't the right time to start having kids. We had a long way to go.

Go to college, get a job before you can think about getting married and having children. Not now. That's what my mum used to tell me. It sucked to be him right now. I felt sorry for Maela and tried to comfort him as much as possible.

It was getting late, so we called it a day and left for home. I had to chew *buai* so mum won't know that I had a few drinks. If mum or Tom smelt the alcohol in my breath, I'd be in big trouble. I arrived home some thirty minutes later feeling slightly dizzy.

My head was pounding but I walked as normally as I could and went straight to my room. I dozed off as soon as my head hit the pillow.

The day before I would fly to Port Moresby, mum wanted us to have a small farewell dinner as a family. She asked me to accompany her to the market. I never really fancied going to the market and shops with mum. Quite often, when she walked into a supermarket, she would spend hours browsing through various goods and noting their prices. She would read the contents and compare prices before settling for an item.

Anyhow, we spent the whole morning going into practically every store in town. I followed mum around feeling my legs hurt. Hours later, and about ten shopping bags in hand, we caught a taxi home. When we arrived home, I threw the bags down, tired as hell. I took a shower and went to my room to get some rest.

That evening, I scraped the coconuts and helped mum to peel the sweet potatoes. She skillfully peeled the sweet potatoes with the non-blade side of a knife. When I tried to imitate her, the potato slipped out of my hand. After many unsuccessful attempts, I managed to peel two, while mum had downsized the hill of sweet potatoes to half.

A grin spread across my mum's face. I couldn't tell whether she was laughing at how inept I was or just enjoying our last moments together.

I reached for the onions and peeled off their flaky skins. As I sliced the first one, my eyes began to sting. My vision became blurry, and my nose started to run. Finally, submitting to the fiery sensation, I reached for a napkin to wipe the tears and blow my nose. I sat up on a stool and watched mum expertly control the knife. As she chopped, she didn't wince once.

Mum cooked the chicken and the vegetables. She made salad and baked a cake. A mouth-watering aroma filled the house. We all sat around the table chatting during dinner. It was a memorable night. I enjoyed the warmth.

After dinner, I went to bed early to get some sleep.

CHAPTER NINE

MY FIRST FLIGHT

I was super excited. It was going to be my first trip on an aeroplane to Port Moresby! All by myself! The check in time at Gurney airport was at eight thirty am.

Mum woke me up at about seven o'clock. I got up, got dressed and had breakfast. Mum had arranged for a taxi the previous day and checked if I was ready.

"I've packed my bags already."

"Have you packed everything you need? Your bag looks too big for all your necessities." She began checking my bag. "Now look at this. What is this? What is it?"

I didn't know whether to answer her or keep quiet but silence was golden, someone once told me. I kept quiet. She waved the condom packet in front of me.

"Am I talking to a stone? I am asking you, Boko. What is this?"

"My stuff!"

"What stuff?"

I looked at the black bag on the table and wondered why mum was so stubborn. There was my personal stuff. I sometimes wondered what kind of a mother I had. She wanted to know everything. She was like a dictator and I didn't have much freedom in school. Now, like this one. Where in the constitution does it say that she had the right to know what I carried in my bag?

However, she was my mum and I knew that such a thing could lead to me getting no pocket money, if any. But what I feared the most was that if I kept quiet, she would continue to search the whole bag and find more.

"Condoms," I mumbled.

She hurled the condom packet into the bin.

"You are going to university to get a degree and not to look for girls! No girlfriends until you have a job and a house of your own."

Why couldn't she understand that I was now an adult? She had a point, though I was irritated by what she sometimes asked.

"The taxi's here. Time to go," mum announced.

I nimbly grabbed my suitcase and backpack and followed her to the taxi. I shook hands and said goodbye to Tom before getting into the cab. Willie and Simon got in the taxi to accompany mum. They also wanted to see me off at the airport.

When we got to the airport, mum and I followed the long queue to get my boarding pass. The terminal at Gurney airport was packed with students who were flying off to various institutions around the country for studies. I shook hands with several of my school mates and congratulated them. We were all on the same flight to Port Moresby. From there, they would catch connection flights.

After getting my boarding pass, I went back to say goodbye to Willie and Simon who were waiting outside the terminal. I hugged both of them for a long time. Mum handed me five hundred kina for my pocket money.

"Love you guys. I'll see you at the end of the year," I said feeling a lump in my throat.

Mum hugged me too. "Love you son. Your cousin brother will be waiting for you at Jackson's airport. You take care and concentrate on your studies."

"I won't let you guys down," I whispered and walked back to the terminal, not wanting to look back.

I passed through the scanners and security, where I had to stop and was scanned again because the alarm went off. But it was just my belt buckle. The tired and annoyed security guard allowed me through to the departure lounge.

"Hi Boko!"

I turned and saw my class girl, Shelma. She was going to the University of Papua New Guinea too. I remembered seeing her name on the acceptance list under the Bachelor of Arts degree course.

"Hi Shelma," I said.

She looked miserable like she had been crying but managed to smile. "How are you?"

"I am fine. I just miss my family already."

"Same here. I'll see you around then."

She walked over to a vacant seat and made herself comfortable. I took a seat at the corner and sat down. Shelma's simple question unsettled me. Deep down I knew that no matter how hard I tried to convince myself that I was fine, life wasn't so fair for me. It's not as if I had never been happy, I had, but the scale of life had always tipped the other side for me.

Growing up with a step father was very challenging at times. I didn't have the best relationship with Tom but I didn't have a horrible one either. Although Tom despised me, I still respected him. After all, he took care of me since I was five years old and treated me like his own son. I hoped to repay him someday.

The boarding call disturbed me from my thoughts and we started boarding the huge Fokker 100 plane. I found my seat, which was a window seat and put my backpack in the overhead locker. I placed the bag containing smoked fish and tulip for my cousin under my seat.

Looking out the window, I saw mum and my younger brothers waving among the crowd. I quickly looked away trying to be strong so I wouldn't cry. I would definitely miss them big time but I also looked forward to the adventures that lay ahead of me.

"Hi, do you need help with the seatbelt?" a female flight attendant asked.

I looked up and smiled confidently at her. "I am fine."

I didn't want to look like a first timer in front of a good looking lady. She had a nice ass, I noticed earlier, when she walked down the cabin aisle to check that all the overhead lockers were closed properly. I figured that she had a nice body under that uniform dress too.

It took me some minutes to stop drooling over her gorgeous body. Seriously, heavenly girls like her were meant to be in places where ordinary guys like me wouldn't find them. One can only dream to have her.

After studying the seat belt for a while, I pushed the buckle together until it made a clicking sound, which I assumed meant that it was secure. I stared at the dull metal clasp resting on my lap. It fastened two separate pieces of navy blue fabric, the ends of which disappeared into either side of my seat. I wondered how much protection it would offer if and when the plane crashed into the side of a mountain in a terrifying explosion of fire and burning fuselage. This was the magical device that was supposed to save me from death, yet it did not offer me even the look of reassurance.

Finding no comfort in the seat belt, I watched the people making their way towards the back seats of the plane. I was amazed that the plane could carry so many people.

"Is this your first time on a plane?" the girl sitting next to me asked.

I regarded her with a quizzical look.

"Yeah," I admitted feeling a little embarrassed.

"Me too," she said with a timid smile. "Oh, my name's Jenny, by the way."

Thankful that I was not alone, I smiled back. "Hi Jenny. Nice to meet you. I am Boko."

She was in another class at Cameron Secondary School. I'd seen her around at school but didn't know her name. We spent the next few minutes getting to know each other. She was accepted to undertake the Bachelor of Education course at the Pacific Adventist University, located just outside of Port Moresby city.

The flight attendants began to go through the emergency and safety procedures as the plane taxied down the runway. I listened attentively to the potentially lifesaving information. I seemed to be the only one doing so. Everyone else were busy chatting away.

I felt the plane lift off the ground suddenly. My heart almost stopped beating. We were ascending towards the clouds. I held my breath for a while. We went higher and higher until the buildings and trees looked so tiny. We were now above the clouds. The alignment of the clouds and the clear blue sky made it look like the plane was not moving.

Some thirty minutes into the flight, the flight attendants served us light refreshments. I enjoyed the small, brown cake and fruit juice. It tasted good. Then, they collected the trash. I was thrilled at the flight attendants doing their jobs proficiently high up in the air.

Apart from some light turbulences that nearly stopped my heart, the rest of the flight went by rather uneventfully. An hour later, the seatbelt sign came on. I hadn't unbuckled my seat belt since take-off.

"Cabin crew, please be seated for landing," the pilot announced on the intercom.

I looked outside the window and saw what looked like Alotau town but much bigger. There were so many houses, roads and high rise buildings. I was terrified and thrilled at the same time. I've heard stories about how big Port Moresby was but now I would be seeing it for real. It was like a dream come true.

The landing was a bit bumpy. I gripped the arm rest tightly as the plane's tyres hit the tarmac, my heart pounded with fear and adrenalin. The plane bounced twice, propelling me forward. Thank god I had my seat belt fastened. Finally, the plane came to a stop in front of a huge terminal. I took a relieving breath and pressed the release button on my seatbelt. I was glad we had a safe flight. I followed the other passengers to the baggage carousel area.

There, I waited with the rest of the passengers, in silence, for our baggage to come around. When my bags finally came around, I collected them quickly and placed them on a trolley. The security guards checked the baggage tags before I headed towards the arrival area anticipating to see my cousin brother, Amin, who would pick me up.

There was a crowd outside the terminal, people waiting for their loved ones who had just arrived. I looked around among the crowd of people for Amin but couldn't find him. I stood for a few more minutes, then went over to a coffee shop nearby to buy a can of coke to pass time. I was more excited to be in Port Moresby than scared of been lost.

After buying a can of coke, I stood around for a while, studying the designs at the Jacksons Airport terminal. I was amazed to see so many advertisement billboards. There were so many people and the terminal was much bigger, much classier and much more crowded than the one at Gurney airport in Alotau. It was a totally new and different world for me.

Amin arrived fifteen minutes later. He found me sitting at one of the benches near the coffee shop and gave me a hug.

"Hi bro. Welcome to Port Moresby."

"Thanks bro. I thought I was lost," I said, feeling relieved.

Amin carried my baggage and the bag containing his smoked fish and tulip towards a Lamana Hotel vehicle. Amin worked as an Accounts Officer there. I got in after him. We drove off, weaving in and out of other vehicles. There were so many buses, taxis, trucks, cars, all rushing back and forth.

Cars whizzed by at high speed and the noisy city traffic was insane. Everything looked exhilarating to me.

It took us a good twenty minutes or so to get to Amin's apartment at North Waigani. Registration at the University of Papua New Guinea would be the following week so I'd be spending the weekend with Amin and his family. His wife, Louisa, was from Mekeo and they had a son, Henson.

"Your *tambu* will arrange a room for you and you make yourself feel at home. I am going back for work. See you in the afternoon," he said before driving off.

"Thanks bro." I waved at him.

Feeling tired, I sat down on a chair and closed my eyes.

CHAPTER TEN

GOLD CLUB – THE PARTY CAPITAL

Back home in Alotau, I rarely went out with friends to the night clubs. My mother was a strict lady. I remembered the time when she found out that I was drunk after following friends to the Jetty at Alotau International Hotel. She gave the green light for Tom to beat me up with a cane. They punished me to sleep outside the house for two nights. Hence, whenever I had a few drinks with friends, I would pretend to be sober when I got home to avoid been caught again.

But for some reason, I was over excited to be in Port Moresby. When Amin asked me to accompany him to Lamana that Friday night, I just jumped into the car without hesitation and we drove off.

At the Waigani traffic lights, Amin leaned forward and turned up the volume of the car stereo. A favorite song was playing and we hummed along while waiting for the traffic lights to turn green. I was already feeling the weekend party vibes.

The Gold Club at Lamana was packed to capacity that night. The club was brightly lit and covered by a thick blanket of white smoke. I squinted as streaks of light circled the room, slowly examining the room in awe. It was much bigger, classier and groovier than all the night clubs in Alotau. In the centre of the room was a large disco ball that shot lights in all directions. Underneath it was the dance floor that was soaked by a sea of people. They would dissolve into a white smoke that shot out from the side of the dance floor. I was on my fifth can of Niugini Ice and already feeling the effects of the alcohol.

I observed a young couple on a table near ours. The man was well dressed, while the lady wore the hottest black dress I had ever seen. After the husband had a few drinks, I saw him heading towards the restroom. The lady kept to herself, sipping her drink.

"Bro, drink your beer," Amin insisted, distracting me.

When I looked back to their table, I saw another man standing at her side. He was clearly flirting with her, and she was just staring at her glass.

Something did not feel right. She said something to the man. The place was really noisy so I couldn't hear what she was said. But it seemed clear that she was trying to reject his advances politely.

Then, after a few minutes the husband returned from the restroom. His face completely changed. I heard the sound of glass been smashed and the husband swearing loudly. His wife looked miserable grabbing his arm and pleading him to stop.

There was no sign of the other man. I leaned over the table and my suspicions were confirmed. He was lying down on the floor, with blood running down his face. The club bouncers came over to stop the furious husband. When people started gathering around them to see what was happening, the husband turned to his wife, yanked her by her arm and they left.

"Hey?" I called out after them.

The husband turned his head around, seething. The wife did not even acknowledge the fact I was addressing her.

"You forgot your purse," I said, stretching out my hand with the small purse.

In a split second he snatched it from my hand and practically ran to the door with his wife trailing behind him.

The bleeding man was helped to the door by the bouncers. He applied pressure to stop the bleeding with a piece of cloth that someone among the crowd of onlookers had given him.

"Gees! I think the lady's husband smashed a glass on his head." I cringed.

"That's his problem. Shit happens all the time here. When a lady says she has a partner, don't push your luck or you'll get into trouble," Amin stated matter-of-factly. "Enjoy your beer bro. I am so proud of you."

"Thanks bro," I said, still shaken by the incident.

Gold Club was his turf and Amin wasn't afraid. He knew all the waitresses, bartenders and bouncers. He signaled a good looking waitress over to our table.

"Samantha, come and meet my small brother. He thinks you're hot."

She blushed. "Amin? Stop it!"

He had a mischievous glint in his eyes. "My brother is your age and single. Just letting you know."

"Okay, I'll think about it. Wished it was my night off," she said nervously and walked off to serve other people.

I was embarrassed. "Idiot! Why did you do that? I have a girlfriend!"

Amin grinned. "Relax bro. She's cool. Did you see her blush? You got her already. She'll come back to our table."

"Where is she from?"

"Central and Milne Bay. One of our *wantok*."

Samantha frequented our table and kept glancing at me throughout the night. She had a slim body with curvy hips and nice breasts. She had an amazing smile. She was gorgeous looking and freakishly resembled Jessica Alba.

"Your brother is having a good time dancing out there. Why aren't you on the dance floor?" Samantha asked when she had a chance to drop by.

"I don't really dance. I mean, I dance. Just you know, not too well," I said, feeling uncomfortable.

"You owe me a dance but not now. Another time when I am free."

She winked and we smiled at each other. I knew she liked me but I still couldn't get rid of Helen from my mind.

Amin ordered more drinks for us with absolute ease since he was a staff. Before I knew it, I was tipsy and in a jovial mood. The loud music mixed with the flashing disco lights made me dizzy.

I was already drunk. Wasted, to be precise. I started dancing up and down the stage and screaming at the DJ upstairs. It was one hell of a night and I had a blast.

CHAPTER ELEVEN

VISIT TO DOWN TOWN

The next morning was hell. My head pounded and my bladder felt like it was about to explode. I forced myself out of bed to use the loo, then grabbed a bottle of cold water from the fridge. My head throbbed from the hangover.

"Good morning *tambu*," Louisa greeted from the kitchen.

She held a cup of coffee between her hands, watching the electric jug boil.

"What time is it?" I asked, slumping into a chair at the living room.

"It's almost ten. You've must have drank too much beer last night." She chuckled. "Coffee?"

"No thanks. I'll just have water."

I gulped a glass of water, feeling the coolness on my throat. I hadn't realized how dehydrated I was until then. I returned to my room to sleep off the rest of my hangover.

After lunch, Amin and his wife decided to show me around the city. I had to learn how to catch the PMV buses before school started. The traffic was horrendous when we got to the central Waigani area.

Amin pointed to a high rise building on the right. "That's the Holiday Inn. It was called the Islander Travel Lodge before."

I observed the hotel with interest and smiled. "Oh, that's mum's favourite hotel."

Mum always told us about her experience at the hotel and the delicious food. Some years back, she was in Port Moresby to attend a church convention. On her return flight, she was offloaded with several other passengers. They complained that they had nowhere to sleep and Air Niugini booked them for the night at the Islander Travel Lodge. They boarded an early bird flight to Alotau the next day.

When the traffic lights turned green, Amin followed the main road towards Boroko. He suddenly stepped hard on the brakes and tooted the horn. A taxi had changed lanes sharply in front of us without giving any signal, almost causing a collision.

"You asshole! Do you know how to drive?" Amin yelled.

It didn't make the taxi driver look back, but at least he had the chance to vent his frustration.

"Bloody uncivilized, highlands idiots! They think they own the road!"

We drove past the crowded Boroko bus stop. There were lots of buses lined up and bus crews were shouting their routes.

"*Tambu*, Boroko is not a safe place. There's a lot of drug bodies and pick-pockets," Louisa warned. "Be careful when you go there. Always put your wallet in your front pocket."

I cringed. "Gee! That's scary."

"Don't go there by yourself. Always go with a friend for your safety," Amin added.

On our way to Taurama, Louisa recounted a story about a thug that used to steal from the commuters at the Boroko bus stop. The public got fed up and one highlands man chopped the thug's right hand off with a bush knife. He was left to bleed to death at the bus stop. Luckily, the police rushed him quickly to the hospital.

"Good one. Serves him right," I muttered.

When we got to Down Town, I blinked my eyes in amazement. The buildings seemed to touch the sky! The view from Crowne Plaza was stunning. It offered a three-sixty degree panorama of Down Town. I looked out to Fisherman Island on my left and the Fairfax harbor on my right. I could see all the way to the wide, open ocean with several container ships waiting for space to berth at the wharves. The tall buildings and skyline were more beautiful in reality than the pictures I had seen in the Paradise inflight magazines.

So this is really Down Town? I am actually seeing it for real. It took me a few seconds to realize that I was actually in Down Town.

"Nice view aye? What do you think bro?" Amin asked.

He probably read it all over my face how ecstatic I was. I fell short of words to describe my experience there. I gave a broad smile to show that I was enjoying myself. We stood there for about fifteen minutes taking in the beautiful scenery before driving down to Ela Beach.

Amin parked the vehicle and we walked down the beach-side pathway. On one side of the path were food and drink stalls and on the other side, benches were set up for people to sit and have their food. We sat down on one of the benches to rest while enjoying the ocean breeze.

There were lots of people at the beach but most of them looked like they were from the highlands. I watched with fascination when some highlanders waded into the sea. They played around in the shallow water, too scared to go further out to the deep. Some boys were playing rugby on the sand. Other kids were playing volleyball and basketball.

"There are so many highlands people in Port Moresby," I commented.

"Oh, they're everywhere in the city. Most of them have nowhere to go because of the tribal fights back at their villages so they build squatter settlements to live in Port Moresby," Amin explained.

"I hope they know how to swim because there's no ocean in the highlands. They might sink like a ship's anchor."

My comment had Amin and Louisa in stitches.

Little Henson was hungry so Amin bought some pieces of lamb flaps and highlands *kaukau* from a barbeque stall nearby to eat before exploring other parts of the city.

We drove along the freeway to Gordon's to check out a second-hand clothing shop there. The low prices caught my eye and I bought several collar t-shirts for school. Louisa spent almost an hour in the shop and came out with two shopping plastics full of clothes. We finally headed back home, feeling exhausted.

To me, it was actually like a mixture of a thrilling movie sequence, a dream and a childhood wish coming true at the same time.

It was an amazing weekend and I wished it could go on forever. However, I couldn't wait to start school at the university.

CHAPTER TWELVE

FRESHMAN YEAR

Enrolment was a lengthy process. I had to go from office to office and follow long queues to get my registration forms signed and stamped. The University of Papua New Guinea's main campus at Waigani was like a town itself. It was huge. After a tiring week of registration, I finally got my room keys from Student Services and moved into the campus on Friday evening.

Some of the boys were drinking that night. They probably had parents who were big shots or business class. Unlike my parents who were low income earners, I didn't have extra money to drink beer. I had had to harvest sea cucumbers with uncle Manoa to assist mum with my school fees. Anyway, everyone had their own life to live and the freedom to do whatever they wanted to do.

Mum had not given me a lot of money. At least, it was enough to buy my stationaries, some clothes, bathing soap, laundry soap and powder.

For a while, I enjoyed the solitude of been on my own. But I started feeling homesick on the second day. It was almost the same feeling that I had on the first day of school at Goilanai Primary School. This was the first time I had to live on my own without mum, Tom, Willie and Simon.

I grew more and more despondent and everything seemed strange. My thoughts wandered back to my family in Alotau. There was no mobile phones back then so I couldn't call mum.

What were they cooking for dinner? Smoked fish and tulip creamed with coconut? What was everyone up to?

I pictured mum sewing or baking buns for breakfast and the boys watching television. I missed home badly.

Home? Do I really have a home with a complete family?

I decided to go for a walk to clear my thoughts. I locked my room door and walked down the street that led to the forum area. There were a few students mingling around. The forum area was the trade center where street vendors would come and secretly sell cigarettes and *buai* to the students.

I stood for a while reading the notices that were on the public noticeboard, then strolled at a leisurely pace past the Michael Somare Library towards the Kuri Dom building which housed the School of Humanities and Business Administration buildings. Since it was Sunday, the buildings were empty. I continued down towards the Ullie Beier building, gulping in the fresh air. It was empty too. Thankful for the peace and quiet, I sat down on a bench outside the Theatre Arts hall.

I wondered where life was going to take me. Where will I end up in life? I thought about how far I've come in life. Why me? I questioned my purpose and wondered why I was sent to this world. Do I have to forget all of my pains and place a mask on my face every day? I searched my mind for peace because I wasn't quite sure where I belonged.

Whenever I asked mum why I was in such a mess, she would say that there are lots of children without a father like me and that I was lucky. Tom was a good man to raise me up as his son. Mum told me that I will always face challenges but it all depends on how I handled them.

Maybe, she was right. Life wasn't easy, and everyone had to find their own ways to cope with the obstacles life threw at them. Even in the depths of my bitterness, I somehow knew that there would be sunny days ahead for me. Although, I didn't have a perfect family, they meant the world to me.

When I got back to my room, I felt a little clear headed. It was six o'clock and most of the boys were making their way down to the mess for dinner.

I quickly showered and put on a comfortable short and a grey t-shirt. I locked my room door and was just about to leave when a guy came out of the room next to mine.

"What time is dinner at the mess?" he asked.

"I think it's open for dinner from five to seven o'clock."

His eyes light up. "Oh okay. Thanks bro. By the way, my name's Duncan. I am from Western Highlands."

"I am Boko Leidimo from Milne Bay."

We both strolled down to the mess. He seemed friendly so it looked like I would be seeing him more often.

I was so excited about starting my first day of classes at university. University was different from secondary school because there was no uniforms. That meant I could wear my favorite jeans and shirts. After breakfast, I made my way to the tutorial room that was given on my timetable for Fundamentals of Accounting class. The lecturer was already in the room so I knocked and waited for a response.

"Yes, come in," the lecturer said.

I was nervous when everyone turned to look at me enter the room. Finding a seat at the back, I quickly settled down. The lecturer handed us the course outline for the semester.

"Get one and pass the rest please," he said. "Now, before I go through the course outline, it'll be good to know everyone by name. I'll introduce myself first and then we'll start with the person on my right."

He introduced himself as Dr. Peter Auka. He completed his first degree in accounting from the University of Papua New Guinea and a masters from the University of Queensland. Then, he went on to complete his doctorate at the Australian National University. Dr. Auka had over twenty years of teaching and research experience.

I was impressed by Dr. Auka's academic qualifications. He stopped talking, and now it was our turn to introduce ourselves. I dreaded public speaking in secondary school. When my turn came, I felt my legs shaking when all eyes turned to me. Some out of curiosity and others out of boredom.

"Hi, my name is Boko Leidimo. I am from Milne Bay province and I last attended Cameron Secondary School in Alotau," I introduced myself quickly and sat down.

"Thanks everyone and welcome to the University of Papua New Guinea, the premier university of the country and the Pacific. Consider it a privilege to be here," Dr. Auka said after all the students introduced themselves. "I am sure, you will all have a great time in your four years of study here.

Remember, university is not for the brainy people but for those who work hard."

Dr. Auka went through the course outline and explained the assessment tasks. After that, he gave a brief introduction about accounting before the class ended.

"So, you're from Milne Bay?"

The young lady in front of me asked. She was a pretty lady, with caramel skin, dreamy eyes and full lips. She had a slightly blonde hair and the rest of her looked fine.

I nodded. "Yeah."

"I'm Natasha Patterson. But, all my friends just call me Tasha."

"Tasha is a cute name."

She blushed. "Thank you."

Our eyes met and held for a few seconds. A spark of sexual attraction was ignited. For a moment, I sat there and observed her. Tasha was tall, which was a plus. I liked tall girls, although I'd never dated one. Most guys liked petite girls. I was no exception. There was something about tall girls that was just sexy.

I enjoyed the short chat with Tasha then packed my notes and left the tutorial room in high spirits.

The first week at the university was not as interesting as I imagined. I made one new friend and met a lady who seemed far too flirtatious for her own good. I also attended all the lectures and tutorials with enthusiasm. I wanted to be there when the lecturer said the first word until when he'd said the last word. I couldn't afford to miss a lecture or tutorial class.

I kept myself occupied with schoolwork, focusing on that rather than the emotional turmoil I was still experiencing.

Education was an excuse to hide my emotions. After all, it was for the sake of education that I left home to be here.

Helen send me several letters. The first two, I sent a reply but I thought she would only prevent me from focusing on my studies so I tried to forget her. Besides, she was far away and I doubted whether she was faithful.

CHAPTER THIRTEEN

LUNCH WITH SAMANTHA

S amantha wanted to catch up for lunch on Saturday. She had asked Amin to pass the message to me. I hadn't thought about her since that crazy night at the Gold Club. I thought of what I was going to wear, and on top of that, was I really about to go to lunch with some random lady I met at a club?

Part of me wondered why I was even bothering to go. I wasn't going to, at first. But then, the thought of Samantha sitting alone at a table, not realizing her date would never show up, just seemed mean.

I decided the least I could do was to hang out with her for lunch as a friend. I was kind of a considerate guy and didn't want to hurt her feelings. I took a quick shower, and wore my blue jeans and a silky t-shirt.

I examined my reflection in the mirror on the back of the closet door. I thought I looked cool. I was tall and didn't have a six pack. So, I guess I could see why there hadn't been a line of girls wanting to date me, but still.

On the bus to central Waigani, I felt apprehensive for some reason. I got off near the Big Roster shop and stood outside for a moment, debating whether I should go in or not. Taking a deep breath, I told myself to relax before entering the cafeteria.

My heart jumped up the minute I caught sight of her. She wore a short, sexy dress showcasing a slim, curvy body and a set of long, lean legs. The kind of legs I wouldn't mind having wrapped around me.

She was sitting by herself, gazing out the window to the busy street, watching people pass by. Taking another self-reassuring breath, I smiled and made my way to her.

She spotted me and waved. A quirky little smile played across her full lips. Samantha really had some rather kissable and enviable lips.

"Hi Samantha." I extended my right hand out to her out of courtesy.

She took my hand eagerly. "I didn't think you'd come."

"Got your message yesterday and didn't want you been stood up," I joked.

"Whatever! Thank you for coming anyway." She rolled her eyes and laughed.

"You look amazing in that dress." I sat down and gazed at her appreciatively.

"Thank you, so do you. I should be jealous, considering the fact that half of the ladies were staring at you when you walked in," she said in a teasing voice.

"Really? I hadn't noticed." I smiled, knowing that she was a little possessive over me.

"I ordered quarter chicken and chips with orange juice. You okay with that?"

"Sounds good," I said.

I noticed that Samantha attracted some appreciative stares from the men in the cafeteria too. One of them was a security guard at the doorway.

"I think someone has a crush on you," I said directing her with my eyes to the doorway.

"What? The security guard? No way. He's too old and ugly for me," she said and slapped my arm.

"Come on, he's human too. By the way, how old are you?"

"Twenty." She pushed some stray hair behind her ear.

"Not bad."

"And how old are you?"

"Nineteen. One year younger than you."

"Oh My Gosh! Hope I won't be charged for child abuse." Samantha screwed her face in disgust as if she had committed a crime.

"Oh? What's the big deal? We're both single and I might be the one abusing you."

That transformed her face. She smiled and her eyes twinkled with a bubbly, carefree laugh. Samantha thanked the waiter when the order was placed on our table and took a sip of the orange drink. "What are you doing tonight?"

I sighed. "I have two assignments to complete."

"Oh sorry. So umm, what course are you taking?"

"Accounting," I murmured, wishing I studied something cool like law or computer science.

"Really? That's pretty cool. You must be really good with numbers?"

"Yeah, I kind of like it."

"Did you always want to be an accountant?"

"Umm, not really. My childhood dream was to be a neurosurgeon but I hated Chemistry and Biology so I took Social Sciences in grade eleven. I was also undecided whether to take law or accounting. I had difficulties remembering dates and events in History class so that's how I decided to apply for accounting on my School Leaver Form," I explained.

Samantha shook her head and laughed. "Oh well, at least you made it to university."

"Thanks, what about you?"

"Well, I actually completed grade twelve last year at Port Moresby International School but didn't make it to university. I flunked Mathematics so I am currently upgrading my marks and been a part time waiter at Lamana Gold Club where we met. I want to be a journalist," she said, sounding unhappy.

"A journalist? That's awesome. You'll be a really good looking reporter on the EMTV news."

"Aaarrgh! I hate Mathematics."

"You can do it Samantha. I'll be around if you need help."

Samantha was a rather down to earth and easy going lady. We had an easy amiable conversation. She told me about her family. She had two brothers and a sister and she was the eldest. Her father was an economist with the Department of Treasury while her mother was a primary school teacher.

"So yeah, I really want to become a journalist, be married by twenty five and have two kids. A boy and a girl," she muttered the last part.

"Sounds like you have everything planned out. We're both young, got a whole life ahead of us."

"What about you?" she asked politely. "Tell me about yourself."

I told Samantha everything about myself and my simple family in Alotau. I also told her about my two fathers.

"So, you've never met your real father?"

"No. I wish I met him."

"I am so sorry darling. Just keep the faith. I am sure you will meet him someday," she said trying to cheer me up.

We barely noticed how fast time flew by. We got carried away with our conversation. Samantha nearly jumped out of her skin when she realized it was almost three o'clock.

She flinched. "I really should get going. I start work at five o'clock."

"I am sorry for taking up your time."

"No, thank you for coming to see me. I had a really good time." She gave a sweet smile.

"You're welcome and thanks for the lunch. You're sweet," I whispered.

"Can I come over to the school tomorrow morning to see you?"

"Sure, Samantha." I nodded in approval.

We walked out to the bus stop, where we stood making small conversation while waiting for a bus. I couldn't stop myself from tucking her hair behind her ear as the wind blew it across her face. I was completely mesmerized by her eyes and really wanted to kiss her right there and then. But I held back because it was too public.

The next day, my girlfriend Samantha visited and we spent the whole day together at the botanical gardens next to the university.

Maybe the term 'girlfriend' was a little too strong. It wasn't like we were exclusive or anything. She was just a no-strings-attached fling. I liked Samantha. A lot. I just didn't want to be in a long-term relationship with her.

At nineteen years old, why should I? I had little to no interest in becoming her or any girl's steady boyfriend. Just the term steady boyfriend freaked me out.

As far as dating was concerned, I told myself that we would just be friends until I saw a future with her. Besides, I still had feelings for Helen.

I'd have plenty of time later in life to settle down and choose a lady to spend eternity with. Like maybe when I was in my late twenties or thirties.

CHAPTER FOURTEEN

AN UNEXPECTED VISITOR

It was another normal day as usual. I woke up, got dressed, had breakfast and headed for the Principles of Management tutorial class. Tutorials where getting boring as hell but I managed to get through without killing myself.

Same frigging routine five days a week! What a bloody monotonous existence!

During Principles of Management tutorial class, Dr. Pious, the lecturer, announced we would need to break up into groups of two for a group project. My partner was none other than Tasha.

There were thirty one students in the class, so there would be fourteen pairs and one which would have three members. I knew only a few students in our class. I saw a forlorn looking guy near the back of the class, thinking he might be the odd one out.

"You don't have a partner?" I asked.

70

He shook his head. "I'll have to find a group who will allow me to join."

"I'm Boko. What's your name?"

"Terry," he said nervously.

"Why don't you join our group? Tasha and I."

His face brightened up immediately. "Thanks Boko. I appreciate that. Thank you."

Terry was a short bloke, had a beard and wore glasses.

"Tasha, I've invited Terry will join us. We could use another Einstein to contribute some ideas," I explained.

Tasha chuckled. "Sure, welcome to our group Terry."

We sat down to discuss the topic given to us. Our group topic was 'Communication and Leadership Skills'. It was due at the end of the semester.

"So, I was thinking maybe we should allocate sections to write about and compile it a week before exams," I suggested.

"That's a good idea. I'll do the introduction part," Tasha said.

"Sure Tasha. Terry, can work you on communication?"

"That's fine with me," Terry said.

"Great! I'll work on leadership and the conclusion," I said.

We were given only twenty minutes discussion time. Dr. Pious asked us to take our seats and he would begin covering the topic for the day. It was going to be a very challenging semester, I thought.

Somewhere in the middle of his lecture, Dr. Pious paused for a while and focused his gaze on me. "Boko, you have a visitor."

"What? Who is it?" I stared at him in surprise.

"You have someone waiting for you outside the room. You have to go see her now," he stated. "You are excused from class for the day."

I wasn't expecting any visitors that day. Still confused, I adhered to Dr. Pious's instruction. Tasha, who was sitting next to me, gave me a questioning look.

"I don't know who the visitor is," I whispered to her.

I packed my stuff immediately and walked out of the room feeling uneasy.

I couldn't make out who it was at first. She was leaning against a brick wall with her back towards the tutorial room door so I could get a glimpse of her from the side. She was short and had a stocky built. She had short, steel-wool hair like the highlanders. I had yet to see her face.

As I started mentally running through the list of girls I knew who were short and stocky, she turned her face, finally revealing her identity.

A mixture of emotions struck me as soon as I realized who she was. I was surprised, confused, excited and scared at the same time. She approached me, grinning from ear to ear. I froze.

"Hi, are you Boko?"

"Yeah," I said awkwardly.

"I am Veronica." Her face beamed and she hugged me.

"Oh, hi Veronica," I said barely showing any expression beside the smile on my face.

"Can we go to the forum area and talk?"

I nodded in agreement. "Sure, let's get out of this place."

On the way up to the forum area, I kept glancing at Veronica. I had seen her in a photograph that Charles sent in one of his letters. She was two years older than me and was in her third year, studying law. Charles had adopted her as his daughter so she was, more-or-less, my half-sister. I couldn't help wonder what my father looked like in person. He'd probably be short and stocky like Veronica, I thought.

"How did you find me?" I asked.

The university was a big place with more than five thousand students and I rarely met some of my school mates from secondary school for days on end. We all had different time tables for classes. Finding someone in such a place was difficult.

"We saw your name in the newspapers in January. We knew which course you were taking so dad told me to look for you when school started," she said. "Daddy knew you'd make it to university."

I glanced at Veronica still confused. "But how did you find me in such a big place?"

"Well, I approached your lecturer and asked if he had a student by the name of Boko Leidimo. At first, he was hesitant to give me any information so I told him everything. I said you were my half-brother and that we have never met since birth. I also said that your father really wants to meet you too. The lecturer was moved and gave me your tutorial time. He told me to pass by the room and when he sees me, he'll excuse you from class to come meet me," she explained in detail.

"You're a genius!" I marveled at her strategy.

Veronica bought me a can of coke and pie from the coffee shop and we found a quiet place to sit down.

"Thanks for the drink and pie." I opened the can of coke and took few gulps.

"You're welcome."

Veronica started telling me about the family in Lae. Dad had told them about me and they were eager to meet me. Courtney was in grade eleven, Bradley in grade nine and the little ones, Amanda, Michael, Pauline and Daphne were all in primary school. She gave me my father's business card and told me to ring him.

"You smoke and chew *buai* right?"

"Yeah." I was embarrassed but admitted.

I began smoking in grade eleven due to peer pressure. All my friends were smokers and I was the odd one out. Not wanting to look uncool, I started smoking without my parents knowing about it.

Veronica bought some cigarettes and *buai* and we chewed. She couldn't stop hugging me from time to time. I knew she was so excited to meet me. I was excited too.

"I'll tell dad that we finally met," she said.

We conversed for almost an hour before Veronica left to attend a lecture.

We ran into each other often at the forum area, and whenever we did, we shared knowing smiles and some light banter. Veronica was affectionate and introduced me to all her highlands girlfriends. I started feeling comfortable with the fact that she was my half-sister and enjoyed her company.

A lot of the highlands girls couldn't believe that I was part Enga because I was tall and looked more like the coastal people. One of them grinned in astonishment. "Wow! Enga and Milne Bay. Such a deadly mix."

"Yeah, I know. I am a hybrid mix."

She cracked up at my sarcasm. I realized that highlanders were generous and warm-hearted people.

Most of the time after our encounters in the library or at the forum area, I left feeling happy. One day, I ran into Veronica and she was smiling with excitement.

"Someone's in a good mood," I said. "What's up?"

"Dad is in town. He flew down from the mine site to do some work at the head office and said to meet you on Friday."

"Oh…"

I stared at her in surprise. I had no idea how to respond.

"Dad wants you to call him," she said.

"Okay, I'll try call him during the week."

"He'll come over to the school see you on Friday evening." She smiled.

"Okay, that would be awesome."

I couldn't believe that I was going to meet my father. Part of me longed to meet him but part of me was scared. I started feeling nervous. I sighed deeply trying to calm my nerves.

That evening, I looked intently at the business card that Veronica had given me again. It had an eye catching logo and layout. It read:

> Charles Tamagu
> Project Manager – Kainantu Operations
> Highlands Pacific Limited
> Head Office Phone: 323 5859

I had had the phone number for a couple of weeks now, but I didn't have the courage to call and talk to him. After lunch the next day, I walked over to the bookshop to use the public phone. Gathering enough courage, I dialed the number on the business card.

323 5859.

I dialed the seven digits quickly so that I wouldn't lose my confidence. Something kept holding me back and my mind kept asking if I was doing the right thing.

The phone rang. I was excited, but nervous at the same time. Excited that I was going to talk to the man I had been hoping to meet for so long, nervous that I was going to speak to the man who was my biological father.

"Highlands Pacific Limited. Hello…"

A young lady's voice answered on the other side of the phone.

"Hello, can I speak to Charles Tamagu?" I said politely.

"One moment please," she said and transferred my call.

I waited patiently feeling my heart beat faster. After several minutes, a man with a deep voice answered.

"Hello. Charles speaking…"

Then it hit me. What would I say?

My hands started shaking and I hung up the phone. I just couldn't gather the courage to say a single word.

CHAPTER FIFTEEN

MOMENT OF TRUTH

We were approaching the end of first semester exams and for once, I was confident of making it to the next semester. Tasha and Terry were going to pass the exam, I was sure. Our group project was submitted before the exams. I was satisfied that we had done an excellent job on it and should get a good grade.

As far as my other courses were concerned, I was reasonably confident that I was going to achieve higher distinctions. Principles of Management was fairly easy. Fundamentals of Accounting required a lot of effort to understand the systematic process from source documents, journals and general ledgers to financial reports. Business Communication was more like a repetition of Language and Literature in secondary school. I was doing fine there as well. I was surprised to find Computer Literacy and Numeracy easy, but that was a relief.

I didn't like the Communication and Life Skills course, but it was the university's requirement to have ninety six credit points to qualify for a degree in four years and that was my ultimate goal. I still had to study and work hard to pass the subjects I was enrolled in.

"Hi Boko, mind if I join you?"

I glanced up to see Tasha smiling graciously. I was sitting on my own at a small table in the mess. That was uncommon. She usually hung out with her gorgeous girlfriends. I didn't know much about her, even after sharing a class with her over the past three months. I remembered her telling me that her father was from New Ireland and her mother was from Central.

"No, of course not. Please take a seat," I invited, indicating an empty chair.

She smiled her thanks and sat down next to me. She was a very pretty young lady. Nice blonde hair, a round, friendly face, and of course, that amazing body. I was a bit infatuated, as I often was around her.

She placed her plate on the table. "You ready for exams?"

"I am not sure but I think I'll scrap through."

"I hope the exams won't be too difficult."

"Yeah, I hope so. We just have to study hard."

"Yeah," she said wryly. "I looked at the second semester outline and I think it's going to be more demanding than the first. I hope we can all cope with it."

"As long as you're around, I'll be fine," I said, grinning.

She blush, probably embarrassed. "Thanks."

I decided to change the subject to avoid causing her any more embarrassment.

"So, I hear New Ireland is a beautiful place?"

She looked up. "Yes, it is paradise. You should visit New Ireland someday."

"Maybe when I marry a lady from there."

She smiled. "Oh, you'll never return to Alotau if you go there."

"Your parents live there?"

"Yeah. My dad is a physician at the hospital in Kavieng."

"So, what's your plan after you get your degree?"

She grimaced. "I haven't decided. What about you?"

"Same here. I'm not sure about my future at all."

"So umm, who was the lucky lady you met the other day?" she asked, staring at me intently.

"She's my half-sister. It's a long story, Tasha."

"I have time," she said, looking at me with a flicker of interest.

I frowned. "Not now, Tasha. I'll tell you later."

"My bad," she said, disappointed by my dismissal. "I am sorry for asking."

She leaned over the edge of the table, exposing her cleavage and a black lacy brassiere. I tried to move my eyes off the sight, but I was too late. Tasha must have seen where I was gawking.

She beamed at me. "I think that's the first time I've ever seen you staring at my boobs."

I gave a guilty smile, not sure how to answer her assertion.

"I ... I'm sorry. I didn't mean to," I stammered.

"That's okay, Boko. You're a cool guy and it's easy to be around you. I'm glad we're in the same group."

"I am, too. You're really helpful. Got to focus on our group project," I said, pretending to be innocent-like.

"And not on my boobs?" She laughed heartily.

"Oh, it's hard enough to avoid staring at you," I said, grinning.

Tasha made me feel at ease about a topic usually off limits. I really didn't wish to continue the discussion, but she raised the flirtatious conversation up a notch.

"So, since you've been secretly staring at me, just what do you see when you look at me?"

"Umm…" I said hesitantly. "I love the color of your hair. It's natural, isn't it?"

"Yes, it's hundred percent natural." She winked at me.

"And, you have a beautiful smile like you just did. It really makes you look like an angel."

Tasha rested her elbows on the table and propped up her chin with her hands. I could see a mischievous look in her eyes, another attractive feature.

"Go on," she said, still showing that wicked smile in her eyes.

I was pretty sure I was been teased, but I didn't know to what end. Yes, I had a girlfriend but that didn't mean I shouldn't enjoy a harmless flirt with other good looking ladies. I put my player mode on.

"Well, you're tall and good looking. I think I liked the top you wore to our first class," I continued.

"Wow! You remembered that. What color was it then?"

"Purple. You looked really good in it."

"You have an eye for details." She smiled in appreciation.

"Well, eyes are for looking. And you are a very attractive lady so I couldn't help noticing you."

"So it isn't just my boobs, then?"

"Oh, no. You're a smart and confident lady with a nice behind."

Many of my male friends teased and reminded me of what a nice ass she had. It was somewhat disturbing to me, obviously, since we were in the same group in class.

"Yeah. I'm told I shake my ass pretty good." She snorted.

"No doubt about it. By the way, how did we get onto this topic? It's getting uncomfortable," I said, feeling uneasy.

"Yes. I know. I can see it in your face. At least, you were man enough to tell me in the face that I am attractive." She grinned, her voice somehow calm and collected.

"Umm, distractingly attractive."

"Well, I suppose I could solve that. I could wear big floppy sweaters, baggy jeans," she said with a raised eyebrow and a cheeky smile. "Then you wouldn't be distracted in class."

I shook my head and laughed. "It wouldn't make the slightest bit of difference to me."

Tasha was one of the popular girls at university. I wondered if she had mistaken me for someone with a higher social standing.

"So when are you going to ask me out for a date?" she asked out of nowhere.

"Well, uhhm I'll be free this weekend," I said. "Do you have anything in particular you would like to do on a date?"

"Be creative. Surprise me!" She challenged.

"Okay, give me a couple of days to work up a plan. How about we meet here again on Saturday and I can make a couple of suggestions and you can pick the one you like."

She laughed, shocked at the idea. "Oh, so its multiple choice, isn't it? I'm impressed. I'll be here for breakfast on

Saturday. In the meantime, I'll see you tomorrow morning as usual in class."

"I'll be there," I promised.

I'd made a promise that I didn't know if I could keep. Coming up with a couple of different ideas for Tasha was going to be a challenge, especially since I didn't know much about her likes and dislikes. I discarded the idea of a movie. That was too easy. I could invite her out to dinner at a nice restaurant. I had some pocket money to spend.

The next day in class, Tasha did something that threw me off guard. As she passed behind me, she rubbed her breasts against my back. It was no accidental contact. It was a deliberate, slow rub. The effect was immediate.

I straightened up and almost turned around. Despite that, I managed to control myself, at least as far as a more visible reaction. It was the less visible one that I had to keep hidden. I knew she was teasing me, but this time she had pushed the game further.

Classes ended at three o'clock on Friday. I went back to my room to take a short nap before dinner at six o'clock. A loud, persistent knock woke me up. Sighing, I rolled out of bed and drowsily put on a t-shirt before opening the door.

Duncan turned with a flicker of smile on his face. "Hey, your sister is outside waiting for you at the car park."

"Oh, okay. Thanks bro."

A mixture of emotions filled my head as I walked out of the dormitory. While actually excited, I was also nervous to meet my real father for the first time.

I made my way to the car park before the nerves started kicking in. Veronica stood with a middle-aged man beside a white Toyota Land cruiser vehicle. My attention was focused on the well-dressed, middle-aged man. He appeared to be in his late forties. He was also short and stocky like Veronica.

His face and beard looked exactly like the photograph mum had given me. However, he was better looking in person, I thought. A wave of excitement and trepidation came over me. What would I say?

"Boko, this is Charles." Veronica introduced him.

He stretched his right hand towards me. "Hi Boko, I am Charles Tamagu."

"Hi…" My voice trembled.

We shook hands silently. Charles studied me from head to toe for a while perhaps questioning if I was his son or not. Then, he smiled sincerely. "How's your studies, son?"

"I am doing okay. Just have exams in a few weeks' time so studying hard to pass," I said cautiously.

"That's good. Both of you concentrate on your studies," he said looking at Veronica, then at me.

"We will pass the exams dad," Veronica assured him.

He opened his wallet and handed one thousand, five hundred kina in notes to me. He also gave Veronica the same amount. "That's your pocket money. If you need anything, call me okay."

"Thank you," I said politely.

Charles said that he had to meet up with his expatriate boss at the hotel before catching an early bird flight to Goroka. He'd be back in Port Moresby in two months' time.

"I'll take both of you out for lunch when I return," he promised.

"Daddy, please drop me off at my dormitory on your way back," Veronica begged. "I don't want to walk back."

"Okay, get on." He turned back to me. "Bye son. You take care and make sure you pass the exams."

"See you at dinner." Veronica grinned.

Charles hugged me before leaving. I wished him a safe flight to Goroka and walked back to my room.

I sat down on my bed for a while thinking about the brief encounter with my father and what it meant. On the whole, I felt a bond that I would always cherish. It filled a vacuum that I had had since childhood. I was reunited with my father for the first time. In time, I really wanted to meet his wife and my half brothers and sisters in Lae.

For now, I was happy to have finally met him. I began to come to terms with how his absence in my life had affected me, and the scars began to heal.

"Okay, I've come up with three options," I said when we met for breakfast on Saturday.

"Three? You went all out, didn't you?" Tasha gasped, as though struck by my ingenuity.

"Well, why don't I tell you what I've come up with and you can tell me which one you prefer."

I went through the list and then sat back to let her consider the options.

"I like all three of them, Boko. I mean, they are all good options. But, they're expensive right? I don't want you blowing a month's budget and having to live on Indomie noodles," she said.

"I have some money to burn. Please pick one option to begin with and we can revisit the others later."

She shook her head. "I don't know which one I like best. They are all good. I'm impressed, Boko."

She sat there, thinking about the options I had proposed.

"Let's put three pieces of paper with a number on them into a box and I'll pick one. A drink date is number one, a dinner date is number two, and a lunch date is number three," she suggested.

I chuckled and took the paper from her, wrote the numbers on the page, tore them in roughly equal parts, folded them and put them in my cap. I shook the cap, then told Tasha to pick one piece of paper. She did so and pulled it out, unfolding it to see what the number was.

"It's number one. Damn! Do I have to dress up?"

"I guess so." I chuckled.

"I can't wait Boko," she said with genuine enthusiasm. "I haven't been on a date since graduation."

"Me too," I lied.

"Really? Why?" She seemed astonished.

"Well, I had a girlfriend in high school but she's now at Divine Word University and we lost touch with each other. I decided to concentrate on my studies to get over her, so I decided to stop dating for a while," I explained to her

She sulked. "And now?"

"Well, I guess the past is history. And truth be told, I think I like you."

She gave an astute look. "Oh, thanks. You're a cool guy, and I like you too."

I think it was that look which gave me more courage than I would normally have. "Cool, let's hang out and see how it goes. You can decide if you think we vibe or not."

"You're going to leave it up to me, are you?" she said with a sneaky expression.

"Yes. The ball's in your court, Tasha. It'll be your decision whether we continue or not."

"Thanks for the confidence in me, Boko." She grinned.

I didn't realize I was staring dreamily at her. Looks and brains are a lethal combination. To me, Tasha had both.

"Going out tonight?"

Duncan was curious when he saw me putting on my shoes. I decided to wear a black jeans with a shirt that had colorful tattoo designs. Studying myself in the mirror, I reckoned I looked good enough to be a model for Stella magazine.

"Something like that." I chuckled.

I grabbed a chocolate biscuit out of the cupboard and shared it with him.

"With Samantha?" he asked.

I shoved a biscuit into my mouth before answering. "No, I have a new date."

His eyebrows shot up in surprise. "You two broke up?"

"Not exactly. Just keeping my options open," I said feeling guilty.

"Oh, you player!" he said with a comical expression.

"Gee, it sounds awful when you put it like that."

Duncan tried to impart unsolicited relationship advice on me so I had to make a quick exit.

"I have to go. I'll be back late bro." I interrupted him.

"Okay. You take care bro," he said disapprovingly.

For some reason, he liked Samantha probably because she bought us *buai* and smoke whenever she visited. He took her side over mine for sure.

I said goodnight to Duncan, locked my room and left. It was already seven o'clock and the girls' dormitories were a few minutes' walk down the street.

Tasha was waiting for me in front of the girls' dormitory. She looked ravishing. She had a tight, black skirt with a white top and wore high heels. It was clear to me, she was not wearing a bra but some sort of sexy camisole under it.

We ended up at the Club Shooters where most of the university students hung out. The club had a spacious dancing floor and played great music. After several drinks, Tasha was in the mood to dance.

"Hey handsome, you owe me a dance," she murmured.

She took my hand and led me to the middle of the floor. A slow song came on which was just perfect. She wrapped her arms around my neck, snuggling into my body. I felt her breasts pressing into my chest as I put my hands on her hips.

She moved back against me in slow erotic movements. I could tell by the sensual movement of her hips that she would be wonderful in bed. The thought of that ran across my mind as we danced together.

I knew I was damn lucky. Tasha had a nice ass. I ran my hands down to grab onto her fleshy rear. I pulled her closer to me and kissed her now faded red lips. She didn't protest as I held the back of her head. Instead, she leaned into me, giving me her mouth for a French kiss.

"You're a good kisser," she groaned.

The song ended and we went back to our table. I ordered another round of drinks and observed the action of the place. People enjoying themselves and women getting hit on by drunk and obnoxious men. One particular guy kept asking to dance with Tasha but after I swore at him to back off, the guy disappeared.

It was past midnight, the time we agreed upon to be back in school. Tasha was already tipsy and continued dancing. I tapped her gently on the back. "Hey babe, it's time to go now."

"Nooo! I want to dance please honey," she groaned.

"Tasha! It's getting late," I said, trying to reason with her.

"Okay, but I'll spend the night with you," she pleaded.

We caught a cab back to the campus and ended up making love in my room. Never before had I experienced such pleasure, and I wanted it to last. Exhausted, we lay in each other's arms.

"Thanks for everything. I had a great time." She snuggled into my arms.

"You're welcome honey." I gave her a quick peck on her forehead and watched her sleep.

CHAPTER SIXTEEN

SOPHOMORE AND SENIOR YEARS

Port Moresby city was definitely a place I never saw myself living in - the crowded shops, the busy streets and traffic, the filth and squatter settlements. It made me sick just thinking about it. I almost got hit by a car several times, got sworn at by angry bus crews and got my wallet that had only twenty kina in it stolen at the Boroko overhead bridge.

Anyways, the first semester was completely shitty. I managed to scrape through with a higher distinction, two distinctions and two credits on my transcript. Then, the second semester came and it was amazing with Tasha. Freshman year was over in October and I flew back to Alotau for holidays.

Willie and Simon couldn't hide their happiness and curiosity. They kept asking questions about life at university and Port Moresby city. We had a special bond. No distance or hateful words would destroy it.

I also realized that Tom had changed. He was friendlier than what he had been before. But he wasn't my father. And he never would be. I had to wonder if this was the same man who mistreated me, the man who mocked me and called me names.

At any rate, I was happy to be home.

The smell of bacon and eggs hit my nostrils as soon as I came out of the bathroom and I instantly felt hungry. Mum was preparing breakfast. I followed the scent to the kitchen, where she stood by the stove, holding onto the pan with one hand and a spatula in the other.

"Good morning mum."

"Morning son." Her voice sounded tense, like something was bothering her.

Taking a seat at the table, I waited patiently for breakfast. Mum finished and served my share on a ceramic plate.

"So you met your father?" she asked in a way that indicated she already knew.

I gave a nonchalant shrug. "Yeah. He came to the school."

"He's actually short. I am taller than him."

"Yeah, he's short. He still has the beard on but I think he looks good with it."

Mum's face brightened up. I guess it brought back some of her fond memories. "And what happened?"

I explained to her what happened, leaving no detail out. There was no use in hiding it. She would have forced it out of me eventually.

I told her about how Veronica found me which eventually led to me meeting Charles and the pocket money he gave me.

The smile on mum's face disappeared and her face reddened slightly like a volcano about to explode.

Don't explode, mum. Please, don't explode. I sighed when our eyes met. It didn't work. "He never spent a kina on you since birth and now he wants to spoil you with money," she snapped. "I don't like how this is going."

I shifted uncomfortably in my chair as I put a forkful of scrambled eggs into my mouth. I could feel her eyes boring into me, like she was waiting for some sort of response.

I snorted, not wanting to discuss about it. "I needed the money for my textbooks and printout of my assignments."

"I know but you might end up loving him more that the man who raised you up since you were a baby. Tom was the one who changed your nappies and washed your *pekpek* with his bare hands. You even *pekpek* and *pispis* on him. Always remember that son," she continued her lecture.

Mum felt the need to remind me in an attempt to pass on what she considered to be much needed wisdom. I swallowed hard. Those words were too heavy for me. I slowly chewed on the bacon and eggs, buying myself some time to think of a way to respond to her.

"Look, I was an innocent and helpless child. According to the United Nations declaration, every child has a right to a home, to be taken care of, fed and clothed," I stated defensively.

Mum shook her head, not buying it. "No matter what your father does, just remember that you owe Tom a lot!"

I suddenly didn't feel like eating anymore and pushed my plate away.

It was a long holiday. School wouldn't resume until March, the following year. I decided to search for a part time job during the holiday period. Soon enough, I was employed by Alotau Family Store and worked for six weeks. I didn't really like the job, but I held on to it as a decent source of income to help me out with my tuition fees. I opened a savings account with Bank South Pacific and saved some of my wages.

The holidays went by quickly and I returned to Port Moresby for sophomore year. Charles stepped in and paid for my tuition fees to assist mum and Tom. Mum gave me some pocket money as well so I was kind of loaded when I began school.

I found out that my father, Charles, wasn't the type that talked a lot but he did care for me. Whenever he was in Port Moresby for work, he would find time to visit me. As usual, he'd take me out for lunch and give me pocket money.

Mobile phones were introduced into the country in the middle of freshman year and began to sell like hotcakes. I was delighted when Charles bought me a Motorola flip-phone and a laptop. The phone had radio, camera, games and internet access. A whole world shrunk into the palm of my hand.

I admit that I was bitter towards Charles for abandoning me from birth. At least, that's what I thought. All I wanted was for my father to bond with me and really understand me. I wanted him to be there for me. Something I missed in my childhood. I was still his son.

I regretted all the harsh things I wrote to him in my letters. I only said them because life was bitter and I was frustrated.

Things were going perfectly with Tasha. We seemed to get along well. But she soon found out from her girlfriends that I was two-timing her with Samantha.

Tasha and Samantha had a heated argument and almost fought the other afternoon when they ran into each other. Tasha went cold on me and didn't want to talk to me. I tried to pretend that everything was fine but I was miserable inside.

I woke up the next morning to the sound of my phone vibrating on the nightstand. Still half-asleep, I reached over and grabbed it. The screen lit up with a picture of Samantha smiling sweetly at me, but I knew that wasn't the case. If I answered it, she would go about swearing and calling me names. Maybe she was calling to apologize for the way she acted the other night. Or maybe she was calling to tell me that it was over.

Either way, it was too early in the day to converse with her. With one swipe of my thumb, the call was ignored.

When I saw what time it was, I groaned. It was already nine o'clock. With a yawn, I forced myself out of the bed and headed to the bathroom for a quick wake up shower.

The shower had done its job and woken me up and I was now ready to conquer the day.

Duncan came over to my room. We became very close like brothers. We shared our lecture notes, food, laundry items and even helped each other with money. Whenever he was loaded, he would sponsor me *buai* and smoke. I did the same too.

"Morning," I said cheerfully.

He made himself comfortable on the chair. "Morning bro."

He asked to use my laptop to type his assignment. I handed it to him and switched on my phone. There was one voicemail from Tasha and a text message from Samantha.

"You're not the guy I thought you were. You'll never be that guy. I decided to stop trying to make you something you clearly are not. Thanks for everything. Goodbye Boko." I sighed when I read Samantha's message.

Duncan peered over his shoulder. "How's things going with Tasha?"

"Not too good bro."

"What happened? You two's make a perfect couple."

"Tasha and Samantha had an argument and almost fought. Now, both of them hate me."

"Oh, that's pretty messed up. Who do you like more?"

"Tasha." I smirked.

"Then, go make it up to her"

Sitting back in my chair, I crossed my arms tightly over my chest and frowned. "And just how do you suppose I 'make it up to her'?"

Duncan shrugged. "That's for you to figure out."

"I have to do this today right?" I asked again.

"Yep. Grow some balls and go talk to her."

"Fine. I'll go talk to her." I sighed.

"You're the man!" Duncan smiled.

I had no idea what I was going to say to her, or how I was going to 'make it up to her'. I was just going to have to wing it and come up with something on the fly.

I came across Wendy, one of Tasha's friends, at the forum area. We had a short chat and she told where to find Tasha. After thanking her, I headed towards the rugby field. It was a five minute stroll.

Tasha was sitting on a form under a shady rain tree, book in hand and sunnies on her face. Her long legs were stretched out in front of her. Surprisingly, she was wearing a top with some sort of funny saying on it. Maybe two-timing her somehow made her question her sense of fashion.

"Hi Tasha," I said, feeling awkward.

"What are you doing here?" She glared at me, her voice was full of venom.

Setting her book down on the form, she sat up and folded her arms across her chest. She was making things more complicated for me.

"I wanted to talk to you."

Tasha removed the sunnies from her face and slid them up to rest on the top of her head. She wanted to make sure I could see her glare loud and clear, with no obstructions. Mission accomplished. I could also see the slight puffiness around her eyes, like she'd spent some hours of the night crying.

She gave a judgmental gaze up and down the entire length of my body. "Talk? What could you possibly want to talk to me about?"

"About whatever that happened and the future of our relationship," I grumbled, becoming increasingly frustrated at the bitchy tone in her voice.

"Talk then." she said, placing her hands on her hips.

It was truth time. I wasn't sure if I was prepared for this. She looked like she was ready to murder somebody. The victim would most likely be me.

"I am sorry about everything. I still want you."

"You what?" She stared at me, expressionless.

"I still love you Tasha," I repeated, suddenly realizing what a dumb idea to say that.

"You love me?" she said, trying to control her anger. "What do you know about love?"

I knew, no answer I gave her would be an acceptable one, so I opted for the truth. "I don't want to be with Samantha."

Tasha closed her eyes as her hands slowly formed into fists at her sides. When she reopened her eyes and they landed on me, I was glad looks couldn't kill.

"Why don't you just go back to your girlfriend?"

"She's not my girlfriend anymore," I said with a defeated sigh, but that only earned me another death glare from her. "Oh well, Samantha thought we were soul mates. But I wasn't serious with her. I didn't want her getting the wrong idea that we're like meant for each other or something."

Tasha chuckled at that, but it was a bizarre chuckle. Like she was about to go insane on me. "If you're not serious about Samantha, why didn't you just break up with her?"

My eyes widened at her suggestion. "I tried to break up with her but she couldn't let me go. So I had to find a way to make her hate me, otherwise she'd make my life a living hell."

Finally, it appeared as though it was all starting to make sense to her. "So, let me get this straight. You dated me to get your girlfriend to hate you for two-timing her, and in turn, you also screwed me up."

"Umm, I guess so. But I really want to be with you."

It did sound kind of awful when she put it that way. Angry tears sprang to her eyes as she threw the book at my chest.

"Go away!" she hissed and gave me her back.

"Look Tasha, I'm sorry, okay? I am not really in the mood for an argument."

Tasha stood still, her back facing me. "You know, I trusted you with all my heart. But you betrayed me. Now, please leave."

When she turned around, I could see she was on the verge of crying and I wanted to disappear, pronto. I would have loved nothing more than to follow through with her request, but I still wanted to give it another try. Problem was, I still had no idea how I was going to do that.

"Let me make this up to you please. Everyone deserves a second chance please," I pleaded.

"I want to be alone, Boko. I want you to leave!"

"Can I get you something? Mud cake? Black forest cake? Cadbury chocolate?" I asked, hoping she'd calm down.

"Leave me the hell alone! JUST GO!" she bellowed, thrusting out her finger in the direction she wanted me to leave.

I headed back to my room totally shattered. I tried to hold myself together, forcing myself to be strong.

"Well? How did it go?" Duncan asked.

I threw myself on the bed and covered my face with my hands. "Terrible! I guess it's over now."

He walked over to sit on the chair beside my bed. "What happened?"

"I explained everything to her. I apologized several times. But she still frigging hates me," I mumbled.

"Gee, that sucks."

"Tasha hates my guts. She hated me before I went over there, and now she hates me even more. I offered her an apology, she didn't accept it. I asked to make up for it, she didn't take it. She wants nothing to do with me, so I can't really offer her anything else. What should I do?"

Duncan shrugged. "You have to come up with something else bro."

My shoulders slumped forward in defeat. I had to come up with something to win her heart. But, for the life of me, I didn't know what to do.

After that, things between Tasha and I went downhill rather swiftly. She refused to answer my calls and ignored all my text messages. She also avoided me in class. The times we had spent together, although brief, were some of the best moments I had at university.

We grew apart and became strangers. Last I heard, she was going out to the clubs frequently with her girlfriends. When I asked her, she shrugged indifferently and said, "You don't own me."

CHAPTER SEVENTEEN

MY FIRST JOB

At seven fifty sharp, I walked into the Deloitte Tower building. The security guards greeted me warmly. I entered an elevator and pressed the button for the fourteenth floor. It was going to be my first day at work. I was tingling with excitement.

After my final semester was over, I had applied to several companies and was offered an internship job as a junior accountant with Price Waterhouse Coopers, a reputable international accounting firm.

The elevator opened and I turned left. I walked down the brightly lit corridor reading the names of several big companies on the glass doors. I stopped in front of a door that had 'Price Waterhouse Coopers'.

Taking a deep breath, I pushed the glass door open. The office was modestly furnished with several work stations and computer screens on them. A reception desk was right next to the door.

An attractive lady smiled sweetly at me. "Hi, how can I help you?"

"Umm, I am Boko Leidimo. I was offered an internship here," I said nervously.

"Oh, hi Boko. I am Marion. We spoke over the phone last week," she said. "Welcome to Price Waterhouse Coopers. We'll have to join the others for a staff meeting. You'll meet your immediate boss later."

Marion locked the main door and I followed her down a corridor of work stations to the conference room. Inside, there were about a dozen men and women. Marion showed me where to sit, then went over to whisper something to the expatriate man at the head of the table. The expatriate man, somewhere in his fifties was my best guess, stood up to speak. He wore an expensive, black suit with a tie.

He thanked everyone present for doing a good job and welcomed me to the team. "Welcome to the team, Boko. Here at Price Waterhouse Coopers, we have an internship program to groom new graduates to be some of the best accountants."

He gave a brief overview of the company and discussed other pressing issues. The meeting took an hour, mostly about numbers and plans. Not much that concerned me. I later found out from Marion that his name was Phil Whiteman. He was the Country Director for the company.

A week into my new job and I settled in nicely. I was attached to the Financial Audits division. The division's manager was a Southern Highlands man. His name was Robert. He seemed to summon me for trivial things. Once, it was for me to fill out paperwork that wasn't even my job. Another time, it was to use me as an errand boy to take some reports to another division. He had a secretary to do that.

The other day, I received a call to go to Robert's office. He handed me a stack of papers. "This wasn't filled out properly, do it again."

He glared as if he had some sort of vendetta against me. I figured he was just creating more work for me. I didn't mind, though. My consolation was the experience it gave me. I was determined to learn as much as I could.

One evening, I finished work late. It was about five o'clock in the afternoon and many of the office workers were rushing to go home. The roads in Down Town had been widened and traffic lights were installed recently to cater for the ever increasing traffic. I stood down the street from the traffic lights waiting to cross over to the bus stop. But seeing how the vehicles were speeding by and knowing how dangerous it was, I decided to walk up to the traffic lights and waited for them to change to red so I could cross.

A scruffy old man, one of the many beggars in town, sat beside the road with his arms outstretched. I pitied him and dropped several one kina coins into the carton placed in front of him. I reached the traffic light area and waited with a group of people. Vehicles sped by sending their obnoxious fumes towards us. After some minutes, the traffic light changed to red and vehicles screeched to a halt behind the white lines except for one vehicle that dashed through, just missing several people who'd started to cross the street.

Several bystanders shouted nasty words at the stupid driver. The commuters in Port Moresby were too seasoned to trust the traffic lights completely.

"Asshole driver!" someone shouted angrily at the driver.

"That type of behavior is why we never move forward," I mumbled.

We crossed briskly to the other side and other people crossed over to our previous side. There were two eateries and the smell emanating from those eateries tingled my nose. The mixture of garlic, lamb, fish and spices made a potent combination. I held my breath for a moment as I walked past feeling the pangs of hunger crawl up in my tummy. I always wondered how the people working inside the eateries could stand the smell. Perhaps, they were used to it.

I made my way quickly towards the crowded bus stop where there were so many people pushing and shoving to get on the buses. I stood patiently at the side not wanting to be in the middle of the crowd. It was common for pickpockets to mingle with the crowd and when commuters rushed for a bus, pickpockets would snatch commuters' *bilums* and bags. I carefully scanned the crowd for any police presence before going over to a highlands man who was standing nearby.

"Bestie, buai stap ah?" I asked.

"Em stap. Wan kina lo wanpla," he replied instantly.

I handed him a two kina note. *"Tupla kam bestie. Kambang wantaim."*

He put his hand into a *bilum* hidden under his shirt and retrieved two betel nuts with mustard and a lime bottle. *Buai* sellers were very discreet with their business activities since the Governor for National Capital District announced a ban on betel nut selling and chewing in Port Moresby city.

I chewed the betel nut, enjoying the light stimulant effect and bought two cigarettes to smoke. The cigarettes made me feel relaxed from the stress at work.

After some time, the crowd lessened and several buses had some seats available. I boarded one of the buses. It was filled in no time and some passengers literally hung onto the door of the bus. I secured a seat beside the window. An attractive working-class lady sat next to me. From her features, I guessed she was from Manus.

Putting on my headphones firmly on my ears, I watched the ocean as we passed Ela Beach on our way towards Koki Market. The afternoon breeze blew straight into my face and I thought back to my village. I would often go down to the beach and watch the beautiful sunset.

The Manus lady tapped me on my arm, breaking into my reverie. "Hey, the bus crew is collecting bus fares."

"Oh, okay."

I took out a one kina coin from my shirt pocket and handed it over to her to pass onto the bus crew.

At Koki Market, several passengers left and new ones hopped on. The bus sped off again towards Badili. There, some passengers got off. A group of men with eyes that clearly looked stoned from marijuana got on. One of them studied the passengers and whispered something to his friend.

The bus slowly climbed up Two Mile hill and one of the men from the group that got on at Badili shouted for the driver to stop. The driver pulled up into the bus stop and almost simultaneously, the men removed sharp, pointed knives from their pockets. The driver and bus crew were caught by surprise. The bus crew had a sharp knife against his throat.

"Hand over all your bags, mobile phones and wallets!" one of the men yelled at the passengers.

Everyone started handing over their possessions. The smallest of the group of men, who looked like he was from Goilala, walked over and tried to pull the bag off the Manus lady sitting next to me.

"Please...please don't take my bag," she begged.

"Give me the damn bag or else..." he threatened her.

His breath smelled of alcohol and many of his teeth were stained with *buai*. The Manus lady kept holding onto her bag and I could tell that the small Goilala man was getting impatient. He suddenly stabbed her in the arm and she screamed out in pain. The other women in the bus started screaming loudly in fear and the robbers panicked.

I was horrified and sat very still, hoping to prevent more bloodshed. Until that moment, I had never known the meaning of fear.

The Goilala man quickly snatched the Manus lady's bag and left the bus. His friends followed and they all ran down the hill towards the Two-Mile settlement. The Manus lady was bleeding badly and in pain. Using her face towel, I applied some pressure to stop the bleeding.

"We have to take her to the hospital. This is an emergency," I said to the driver.

The driver nodded in agreement and we headed off towards the Port Moresby General Hospital. I turned back to the lady and asked for her name and if she wanted any of her family members to know about her condition. Luckily for me, the robbers didn't get to me and I still had my phone.

"My name is Angela. Please call my mum," she told me her mum's number.

I called Angela's mum and told her about her daughter and the incident. I also informed her that Angela would be dropped off at the hospital.

After hanging up, I studied Angela. "You'll be okay on your own until your parents arrive?"

She kept sobbing and her eyes were filled with tears. "Can you stay with me please?"

I was starving and couldn't wait to get home and have dinner. But the poor lady looked so helpless and I couldn't leave her. When we arrived at the hospital, I helped her out of the bus and to the emergency area. There was a long queue of patients and people there.

I struck up a conversation with Angela, asking where she lived and worked. She answered all of my questions, never taking her eyes off me.

It was going to be a long night ahead. I sighed, feeling hungry.

A week later after the incident, I was busy working on a client's audit report when my mobile phone rang. It was a new number. I didn't like entertaining unknown numbers so decided to let in ring out. Some people didn't check their numbers properly and dial the wrong numbers.

My phone kept ringing and I got really annoyed. "Yes! Who is this?"

"Hi," a female voice said. "Is this Boko?"

"Yes, and you are?"

"Hi Boko. Hope I am not disturbing you. It's me Angela from the bus incident."

I remembered giving Angela my mobile number when she asked at the hospital.

I calmed down "Hi Angela. How's your arm?"

"Still sore but I am okay. Hey, you wanna hang out for lunch with me? My treat."

"Okay... I mean sure."

"That's if you're single."

"What?" I was caught off guard with that remark.

"You scared? I don't bite."

I smiled at my computer like an idiot. "See you at lunch time then."

When I met Angela at lunch time, I gasped.

She had definitely dressed to kill in an executive suit that clung to her shapely figure. She looked stunning and sophisticated. I couldn't believe it was the same helpless lady I had met on the bus. If only looks could kill, I would be dead already. In front of me was an angel. Totally.

"Wow!" I said before I could stop myself. "You look ravishing."

"Thank you." She blushed and her pretty face turned a little red.

"So where will we have lunch?"

"I wanted to surprise you." She signaled a cab to stop.

"I hate surprises!" I sighed and jumped into the front seat of the cab.

She smiled. "You'll see. Just chill honey."

After five minutes, we arrived at the Ela Beach Hotel. We found a table beside the pool. Angela ordered meat lovers pizza together with orange juice. I could see why she chose to come here. The hotel was cozy, the food was delicious and the service was first-class. I was actually impressed.

We chatted and laughed all through lunch. I couldn't believe how time flew. It seemed like she didn't want lunch to end either.

As we stumbled out of the hotel, she held my hand. I loved it. Everything about Angela bewitched me. In the taxi, I found myself sitting next to her with our thighs touching. It had been a while since I had been with a lady, and I was nervous about the physical intimacy. We exchanged a series of shy smiles.

I couldn't help wondering what it would be like to kiss her, watch her lie in my arms or make love to her. An angel like her, half naked in skimpy lingerie piqued my imagination and I could feel my pulse racing. I snapped back to reality when we reached the bus stop in town and got off the cab.

"Thanks for the treat. I had a great time."

"You're welcome," she whispered. "I'd like to see you again."

"I'll think about it." I teased.

She pinched me gently on the side. "Come on. Say yes please!"

"Yes, I'd love to see you again."

She winked. I liked her a lot. Not really love, just a nice connection.

CHAPTER EIGHTEEN

AN OVERPROTECTIVE MOTHER

After lunch, the day passed by rather slowly. I was working on a report when my phone started ringing. I hurriedly answered it without checking the identity of the caller.

"Boko?" Mum's voice echoed. "Why aren't you answering my calls?"

Though she was in her forties, her accent was still strong, and her tone of voice had not gotten any softer or nicer.

"I'm at work mum."

"I have been calling you since morning! Do you even care if I died?" Her voice was laced with anger.

"You're obviously not dead." I smirked.

"So, you don't have time to talk to your mother?" Mum apparently ignored my smartass remark as usual.

"I've been busy mum, working, you know."

Mum didn't even care enough to let it bother her. "Work? Your family is more important than your stupid job!"

"Mum, what do you want? Money? Do you need money?" I rubbed my forehead in exasperation. Though, I was not new to mum's dictatorial attitude, she still managed to get right under my skin.

"Your father and I argued about your graduation. He suggested for you to go over to Lae for the weekend right after your graduation. He said to arrange for two pigs to make a *mumu* for you."

I smiled with excitement. "I'd love to go over to Lae to meet my family there."

"No, you're not going! Charles has his other kids to spend his money on, not you. Your family are the ones here in Alotau, not those people in Lae!"

Since childhood, mum had very high expectations of me and I had to live up to them. I sometimes hated her for trying to control my life. I wasn't a kid anymore.

"Mum, are you out of your mind? He paid for my tuition fees from second year to final year so I owe him too."

She cut in abruptly. "You are not going and that's final!"

"I am not a bloody kid anymore. I am capable of making my own decisions!" I yelled.

"Who do you think you are talking to Boko? Huh?"

"Look mum…" I tried to reason things out.

The witch wouldn't even let me finish. "Yes, I am your mother! And I know what's best for you!"

"Best for me?" I was livid at her reasoning. "You only want me to do what's best for you! You're a self-centered person and have too much ego. You can't accept the fact that I have a father who cares about me too!"

It felt damn good to finally say that to her. I had thought of it before but didn't have the guts to tell her.

"Where did you get your courage from to talk back at me? You have forgotten who you are, your family and how you got to be where you are now! So, you think you're working for money and you can do whatever you want huh?"

"I haven't forgotten but I am sick and tired of you controlling my life!"

"You either follow what I tell you or don't ever come back to Iyaupolo! Don't make me call on my mother's spirit to banish you and you'll be cursed all your life!"

"What? Are you disowning me?" I twitched my eyebrows in surprise.

"You're not going to Lae! Do you hear me? You will listen to me and you will obey me! I am your mother! It's because of me, you're a man now!"

She hung up without an 'I love you' or even good bye. I banged the phone on the table in complete disgust. Wasn't mum just lovely?

My afternoon was ruined. After work, I went straight home and crashed, without having dinner. I woke up later that night, cooked dinner and checked my phone. There were about ten missed calls along with several messages. Sighing, I went through the recent call list. There were two missed calls from Angela, the rest were from Charles. Frowning, I quickly called my father's number back.

"Hello?" I mumbled.

"Good night son. I tried calling earlier but it went straight to voicemail." He sounded unhappy.

"Uh yes, sorry, I was tired and dozed off after work."

"That's okay. I wanted to talk to you about your mother. I don't know why she can't allow you to come over to Lae to visit your other family here after graduation."

"She's getting old and sometimes doesn't think straight."

"I think she's just over protective because she raised you up so I don't have much say. You're an adult now so you make your own decisions about your future. Son, always remember that you have two families."

Charles thought mum was manipulating me to disown him and the family in Lae. To some extent, he was right.

"I won't forget. Are you still coming over for my graduation in March?" I asked hesitantly.

"I really don't want to run into your mum and dad. I won't promise you anything."

For some strange reason that I couldn't understand, my life seemed to be turning upside down again. Everything was just getting blown to hell. I closed my eyes and leaned my weary head against the window. Stay strong, stay calm, stay positive, I told myself.

Angela and I dated for a few months. She was a twenty five year old lady with her five year old son, Jayden. She had decided to walk out of an abusive relationship. I was hesitant at first and I wasn't sure if I was ready to play a fatherly role to her son. However, inexorably, her seductive spell trapped me. Needless to say, I kept an open mind, and took the chance on getting to know her. Almost instantly, I felt a strong connection with her and quickly put aside the fact that her son would be a part of our relationship as well.

She would bring her son, Jayden, by my apartment and the three of us would hang out. He was in elementary school and we picked him up one afternoon. He was a chatterbox and interested in who I was. He seemed quite smart for his age and his interest in how things worked impressed me.

Before I knew it, I was watching cartoon shows, taking Jayden to the park and spending time with him when Angela was at work or out shopping.

CHAPTER NINETEEN

NOT READY TO BE A FATHER

Ten missed calls.

I stared at the notifications on my phone screen. Putting down my cup of coffee, I picked up the phone, debating whether to call Angela or not.

I had ignored all her calls and every text message she had sent me over the past week. I just didn't know how to reply to her anymore.

"Boko, pick up the phone. We need to talk about this."

That was the last text message Angela sent me, five days ago. When she first told me the news, I was shocked. We took every precaution. I got so pissed I overreacted. I wasn't ready for a baby and I knew mum would go berserk if I told her.

Angela was the matured one in our relationship. She tried to calm me, promised me it would be okay and that we would figure it out. But at twenty two, I was so focused on enjoying my life and climbing up the corporate hierarchy. I walked away and ignored her calls thereafter.

"Boko?"

A soft voice made me look up.

Marion, the receptionist, reminded me so much of Angela at first glance. She smiled politely. She was a friendly lady who dropped by my desk occasionally to chat.

"Yes Marion, what can I do for you?" I responded, trying to remain professional.

"Are you okay?" she asked, studying me.

Marion had no idea how much of an impact her question had. A pain grew in my chest. History was repeating itself. I was running away from my own child, just like my father. I tried to detach myself from my emotions but it was simply not possible.

"Not too good," I murmured.

The guilt on my face must have given away the fact there was more to it.

"Take it easy Boko," she said and returned to her table.

I had to complete my reports or face the wrath of my bosses. There were three emails in my inbox. Two were spam messages. God knows why the company paid for a spam filter! The other email was about a new contract to provide taxation services for a catering company. I tried to work on my reports but couldn't concentrate. My conscience tormented me and it was beginning to wear me down.

After work, I caught a thirty minute ride by cab to Angela's apartment. As I approached her apartment gate, I began to consider what to say. I was afraid of facing my own pregnant girlfriend.

What if she wasn't home? What if she didn't want to see me?

I kept walking and before my thoughts got too out of control, I was in front of her door. I took a deep breath, anxious for what was to come. There was no turning back now.

I knocked on the door and waited patiently. Everything seemed obscure and pretty messed up. My legs stumbled.

Grow some balls and don't run!

I almost didn't notice Angela as the door opened and she appeared in front of me.

"Boko?"

It sounded as though she was both surprised and questioning why I was there. I took in a deep breath. My gaze drifted from her eyes to her abdomen. It wasn't bulging but looking at it made my own stomach twist.

"Hi Angela." I swallowed hard and ran a hand through my hair. Another nervous moment.

Angela would have smiled at my awkwardness, but the situation that brought us together prevented it. Instead, she stepped aside and welcomed me into her apartment. I wondered if she even knew why I was there.

As I took a seat and waited for her to sit next to me, I organized my thoughts. She positioned herself on the other end of the couch. I could tell she too was very deep in thought.

"I want the child and I want to be with you," I said, breaking the silence.

Angela bit her lip, looking down at the floor. I guessed she was considering not taking me back. She could manage on her own and didn't need me. I didn't blame her. She must have spent the last week full of anxiety, trying to plan what her future would be like. Despite her hesitation, I was prepared to support her now, regardless of how long it took for her to forgive me.

"I had an abortion," she announced before I could go on further.

I was dumbfounded. My thoughts burnt like fire, spreading to my chest and stomach and I suddenly felt nauseated. I must have heard wrong.

"What?" I had to ask.

Angela shifted closer to me. She put her hand on my knee and spoke softly. "I just... I just couldn't do it alone."

The words struck me like another explosion in my core. I didn't deserve this woman. She comforted me while I sat there speechless. I gazed into her deep brown eyes and saw my own reflection. A scared, irresponsible man.

"I'm sorry." I lowered my head in remorse and shame.

Tears built up in Angela's eyes. I felt her hand shake and in one moment, she completely broke down. She put her face in her hands and trembled as her emotions took over. I wondered how many times she broke down, while I avoided her calls.

I couldn't take it any longer. I took her into my arms and pulled her onto my lap. As I embraced her, she leaned her head on my chest. I knew I had let her down.

"I am sorry," I murmured again, not knowing what else to say.

Eventually, our differences outweighed the positives in our relationship and we had to call it quits. Not only did I spend a few months as a 'father figure' to Jayden, I'm grateful that he had taught me a lot. Jayden showed me what unconditional love was. I finally understood how it felt like to be a step-father like Tom.

Angela and I managed to remain on good terms. We decided to move on, but every now and then when we bumped into each other, she'd always manage a hello. It was comforting to know that there were no negative feelings, but I longed for the affection she'd once shown me.

CHAPTER TWENTY

THE REUNION

BEEP! BEEP! BEEP! 8:00 AM!
The alarm robbed me of my sleep. As usual, I forced myself out of bed and languidly made my way to the shower. I hated Monday mornings. I dreaded going to work again after a weekend that had passed by so quickly.

I slowly brushed my teeth, took a shower and changed into the company uniform. I wasn't too keen on wearing it but it was company policy. I received a call from Robert some minutes after I arrived in the office. I was about to log into my computer.

"Morning Boko, are you in the office?"

"Yes boss. I came in at nine o'clock," I answered. The words came out of my mouth automatically. It was something I said almost every Monday morning.

"Have you completed the reports for our clients?"

"Not yet. I should complete it today and email it over by this afternoon," I said. Again it was a response that needed no thinking.

"Ok then, Boko. I won't be coming to the office today. However, I'll work from home. Please email me the end of the month reports. I'll come to work tomorrow," he said in a commanding fashion.

"Asshole!"

I swore after ending the call. Working from home was a lame excuse. As if Robert even worked at home. He would probably check his emails twice and enjoy the rest of the day. It doesn't take an hour to check emails. If only this work from home opportunity could be given to us interns as well.

Knowing that my boss wouldn't be in for work, I went over to the cafeteria to have my breakfast and buy *buai* from the street vendors. I returned to my workstation at around eleven o'clock, after breaking the Guinness Book of World Records for the slowest time to finish a sandwich.

I turned on my computer to check my emails. There were five new emails. The first email was another one of those junk mails. I double clicked on the second email since it was marked as High Priority. It was from Phil Whiteman to Robert and copied to me to provide the financial reports for the past month.

I scrolled down further to check the last three emails. Two of the emails were from Robert. The first one notified me to complete a spreadsheet which needs to be sent to the project team immediately. The second email informed me to fill another sheet with the details of what work I did hour by hour in the entire day. I had to send it back to him before close of business. I would need to make something up to fill that second sheet.

Finally, I opened the last email which read: 'Reunion of all former Cameron Secondary School graduands of 2002'. Thrilled, I read through the email. It was from Jacob, a former class mate from secondary school. He was requesting for all former grade twelve students of Cameron Secondary School that graduated in 2002 and now residing in Port Moresby to meet at the Natures Park on Saturday.

It was a group email so I checked all the email addresses it was sent to. One particular address caught my attention.

My heart skipped a few beats.

On Saturday morning, I woke up early and got dressed. It was the reunion day, and I was exhilarated. I decided to wear a faded jeans with a silky t-shirt. I liked the faded jeans. It was the latest trend and I thought it made me look fashionable.

At the Nature's Park, I met up with my former school mates. Sebastian and Leonie were in the same class and now engaged. Sheila was dating Chris. Most of us were still single though. I went around greeting everyone. Then I noticed her!

She looked even more beautiful than I recalled. A bulging tummy was evident. I knew Helen would come but I was not expecting her to be pregnant. A feeling that I never expected came over me. Jealousy. Anger. Envy. Regret. I still loved her but my heart sank. Soothing myself down, I regained my composure and strolled over to meet her.

"Hi Helen. It's nice to see you after a long time," I said pretending to sound casual. "How are you? I mean, how's life?"

"Hi Boko. I am fine. It's good to finally see you after what? Four years? You're looking great too."

We stood there for a long time, catching up on the past. Her family relocated to Madang because her father was offered a job with PNG Power Limited there after our grade twelve graduation. She continued her education at Divine Word University attaining a Diploma in Tourism and Hospitality. After graduation, she got a job at Qantas Airlines.

"So umm, you're married right?" I asked hesitantly.

"No, not yet. We're just living together."

"And where is my *tambu* now?" I grinned wryly.

"Can we talk about something else?" Helen shot me with an annoyed glance.

"Oh, I am sorry. I'm just happy to see you again. You know, I missed you."

She gazed down and her normally light brown cheeks seemed flushed. "I still love you Boko. I love you much more than my hubby, but it's too late."

"Why didn't you wait for me?" I sighed.

"Oh, come on. That's not fair. I waited for your reply to my letters but they never came. I thought you found someone new and forgot about me," she said, trying her best not to cry.

I regretted not replying to her letters, for trying to forget the love we had for each other.

"You look beautiful just like the first time I laid eyes on you back in school," I said.

"Boko, I still love you and I want you, but I am five months pregnant." She gazed at me with pleading eyes.

"Oh well, congratulations and best wishes Helen. I am not planning to ruin your marriage. I'm sorry. I have to go."

"No! Wait…" She pulled me towards her and the next thing I knew, she kissed me on my lips. "That's for all those years I waited for you."

"You know, you've just cheated on your hubby. Let's just forget about each other again."

"I can't…" she murmured. "I will always love you."

Tears began to form in her eyes. I walked away trying to be strong but inside, my heart was torn into a thousand pieces. I couldn't erase her from my mind. To erase the happy memories, the laughter and the love that we had was not easy. But the worst thing was realizing that I would never have her again.

It was all supposed to be so easy. Marry my secondary school sweetheart, buy a house, have as many children as physically possible and patiently work for somebody else until my dream of owning an accounting firm became a reality. It was a perfect plan.

Now five years later, I had a good job and everything was going according to plan, until I met Helen again. The reunion didn't turn out the way I expected it to be.

I always thought that Helen was my soul mate. Maybe I was wrong. Maybe, she wasn't meant to be my wife. Should I forget Helen? Or should I try to get back with Angela or Tasha?

For a week or so, I was really heart broken. I felt like there was no meaning to my life. It was like pieces of broken glass, jagged pieces surrounding my heart. Every time I breathed, they stabbed viciously at me, incapacitating me and making me wish I was dead.

My life became a blur and I welcomed it with open arms. It was just too painful. It actually took me more than two weeks before I finally realized that there was no such thing as 'happily ever after'.

CHAPTER TWENTY ONE

REKINDLING OLD FLAMES

My graduation day was around the corner. For the past month, mum had been calling me almost every second day. Well, no good news ever came from that.

I was sitting outside on the veranda of my two bedroom apartment soaking up the scenery of the night sky. Staring at nothing in particular, I debated whether or not to ring mum and find out what she wanted. I lit a Pall Mall red cigarette and puffed deeply. The effect of the nicotine gave me a relaxed feeling. I wasn't worried about her health, since the old woman was still fit as a fiddle and could easily be mistaken for someone in her early thirties.

The shrill beeping from my mobile phone interrupted my brooding thoughts. I frowned, wondering who was texting me at such a time. The glowing numbers of the digital clock on the phone told me it was nearing two am. I supposed on a

Friday night, it wasn't completely unusual for people to still be out and about.

I quickly checked my messages and was slightly surprised to see a new number. The number didn't appear familiar either. Feeling curious, I opened it.

"Hi, you still up?"

I sat staring at the mobile phone's softly glowing screen. I didn't like responding to strangers. But this person seemed to need some sort of response and he or she wasn't going to get it unless I texted back. I quickly typed a response and pressed send.

"Hi. I am sorry, but who are you? You probably texted the wrong number."

I flicked the cigarette butt to the flower garden below and headed to my room. I jumped into bed and tucked my legs under the silky bed cover. Free from worries momentarily, I decided it was time to get some beauty sleep. As I was reaching over to switch off the light, my phone beeped again. Whoever it was had replied back. I picked it up.

"Oops! My bad. Last time I checked this was Boko's number. Tasha."

My heart soared. Could this be true? I stared at the phone in disbelief. Tasha rekindled memories that I had tried to hide somewhere in my mind. I quickly typed my response, feeling my heart beating faster.

"Hi Tasha. What's up at your end?"

After three minutes of silence, I came to the conclusion I wasn't getting a text back and sighed. The shrill beep of the phone disturbed me again. I read the message.

"Went out with girlfriends from work. Had a few drinks and just got back home. So many things on my mind and can't sleep."

"You okay?" I had a giddy feeling when I pressed send.

"What do you care? What is love to you? What does marriage even mean? To me, it's all temporary."

I pondered over her questions for some minutes and typed a sarcastic answer.

"Love is when you sign a death warrant and marriage is when you compromise some of your dreams and aspirations to make another person happy."

"It's a total waste of time!"

"Why are you so negative?"

"I am not been negative. I am just protecting myself. I like my solitude."

I was tempted to type a sardonic reply like 'why text me if you like your solitude' but decided not to. It might cause unnecessary drama and that was the last thing I expected. Instead, I played reverse psychology in my response.

"One glorious day, you'll wake up and realize you're forty and still single with five kittens to keep you company and a hard drive full of romantic movies to entertain you."

"And that day, I will definitely think of a wonderful guy I once met at university. He stole my heart for a while and then broke it! I'll tell my kittens about him."

I laughed quietly at her frivolous response. "I am sorry. Do you want me to leave you alone?"

I had never really thought she was going to give me a second chance. I slumped back into my fluffy pillows, stretched my arms as I waited for her response.

"Please talk to me. I don't know why I've been thinking a lot about you lately. My heart wants you back but my head doesn't."

I smiled slightly. She was actually considering a second chance. I had been single for a month now. A few ladies asked me out, but I was emotionally unavailable.

I texted after a few minutes of silence. "I missed you, Tasha. I understand you're mad and I am truly sorry. Whatever happened is history. I am not trying to make excuses but I just want to try again."

"I missed you too. But if you ever break my heart again, I will kill you. And I mean it."

We texted for almost an hour before calling it a night. I put my phone on silent mode and switched off the light. Feeling happier than I had in weeks, I dozed off immediately.

Another week went by. Tasha suggested to meet up for dinner at the Italian restaurant at Lamana hotel on Friday. The restaurant was the best in the city and busy as usual, but she loved the food there.

At half past five, I walked out of my office. A heavy downpour began as I made my way to the bus stop, soaking my long trousers and hair. I caught a cab from Down Town to Waigani where the restaurant was located. The wet roads reflected a blaze of color. Red car tail lights, orange street lights and the white headlights.

I planned to wait outside the restaurant but drying off in a comfortable chair became much more appealing. The delicious aromas of the food greeted me as I opened the door; ginger, garlic and spices. A waiter escorted me to my table. After twenty minutes, I began to feel impatient and asked for the menu, to provide both something to read and a distraction to pass time.

Every time the door opened I glanced up eagerly, only to be disappointed on each occasion. The restaurant began to fill and my despondency grew. By quarter past seven I began to think I would be eating alone. At half past seven, I had another glass of vodka and thought of going home. I decided to wait another thirty minutes.

A few minutes after eight, the door opened and a bedraggled figure appeared, shaking an umbrella and dripping water from a raincoat. It appeared like a woman, but the raincoat hid her face. I watched her remove the wet raincoat.

Tasha Patterson!

I waved at her across the room and received an answering wave with a broad smile. She wore a tight dress, accentuating her voluptuous figure. As she approached my table, I realised for the first time what I was missing. She was a goddess!

"Hey Boko." She smiled, her eyes seeming to sparkle. "God, isn't this weather awful? It took me ages to find a cab."

"I know, I had an awful journey here too," I mumbled.

"I finished really late and had to go home before coming here," she explained.

I pulled out her chair and she sat gracefully. I was pleased the night would not be a complete disaster. I noticed Tasha had a tattoo of a rose on her right leg. It was actually kind of cute and sexy.

"Nice tattoo," I said, hoping we wouldn't be discussing work.

"Thank you, I got it inked a month ago."

During dinner, the conversation changed to more serious stuff. Tasha was still hurt but she wanted to give it another try.

"I want you to meet my parents," she said in a serious tone. "We have to take our relationship to the next level."

I was stunned. "Okay…"

"My father is a very protective man," she warned. "Just letting you know in advance."

"It's okay Tasha. I'll meet them whenever you are ready."

I was thrilled and nervous at the same time. I just hoped Tasha's parents would approve of me dating their daughter.

CHAPTER TWENTY TWO

A RAY OF SUNSHINE

Ever since the day I enrolled at the University of Papua New Guinea, it had existed on my mind. I was only eighteen years old when I entered university.

It was like a dream. At times it was like a ray of hope. A ray that sometimes, poor grades dimmed along the way. A ray that grew brighter with every new semester. A ray that had grown into sunshine.

Mum and Tom had travelled to Port Moresby to witness my graduation. Mum was so proud of me wearing the blue gown and the man I've grown up to be. She had a radiant smile on her face.

The sight at the University of Papua New Guinea Drill Hall was like a sea of blue gowns. The graduating students, all from different schools now appeared alike. The scorching sun couldn't erase the smile on their faces. Blazers, suits and ties, everyone had a million and one reasons to be proud. The emotions were next level.

Memories of every moment of my life on campus came flashing back. Examinations periods and everything that came with it. The times when we had no money. The times when we boycotted classes in protest over political issues, and the friendship. I thought of all the sleepless nights, energized by coffee and Snax biscuits or Indomie noodles to complete my assignments and smiled.

The long procession was led by the Chancellor and the Vice Chancellor. A huge crowd of family and friends gave us a standing ovation before we took our seats. After an inspiring speech by the guest speaker and the Vice Chancellor, we were conferred with our respective degrees.

Hugs, laughter, tears and clicking of cameras followed I hugged and congratulated Duncan for attaining his law degree. He was one of the first people I met at university and we remained best friends for four solid years. I also congratulated Terry, my course mate. We took photographs together before joining our families.

"I am so proud of you and everything you have accomplished. My heart is completely overwhelmed with love for you, my son," mum said in tears.

That was the moment that broke me. Tears of happiness trailed down my face. I was over the moon. It was by far, the proudest moment of my life.

Wiping my tears, I gave the scroll containing my degree to mum and walked over to find Tasha. She was taking photographs with her family. Our eyes met and she threw herself into my arms. I embraced her for a long time.

"Congratulations gorgeous," I whispered.

"Thanks handsome. Congratulations to you too."

I could feel Tasha's parents' eyes on me. The look of surprise and query on her father's face intensified. We exchanged unsure glances. I let go off Tasha.

Tasha's mum studied me, as if trying to figure out what my deal was. I'm sure it was shocking enough for her to see her daughter hug a guy so intimately. I had to be blowing her mind right then. I studied her, an older version of Tasha.

"Dad...Mum. This is my boyfriend, Boko," Tasha said nervously.

I took a deep breath and smiled charmingly at her parents. "Hi Mr. and Mrs. Patterson. Nice to meet you."

"Hello Boko," Mr. Patterson said in a stern voice. "We've heard about you. You better take good care of my daughter."

"And please, don't you ever break her heart again," Mrs. Patterson added.

"I'll try not to hurt her, ma'am," I said nervously.

"You're welcome to visit us anytime, young man. It would be nice to spend a Christmas vacation with us in Kavieng."

"Thank you, Mrs. Patterson." I sighed in relief.

At least, they knew who their daughter was dating. Tasha had a permanent smile on her face. I hadn't realized how much her parents' acceptance meant to her until then.

I took Tasha over to meet mum and Tom. While mum and Tasha were busy chattering about the graduation and how happy they were, my phone vibrated. It was a message from my father, Charles.

"Hi son, I am right at the back. I can't come to you because your parents are there with you. I can only watch from a distance. Just know that I am so proud of you. You've made it! Congratulations and much love. Charles."

I turned and quietly scanned the crowd for my father. He waved at me from the back. I acknowledged him, feeling a surge of gratification. I was overwhelmed when I saw how proud and happy he looked. I owed him my success, my heritage and the bond with both families. In the short time I spent with him, I found and felt a different kind of love. One that was not judgemental. A love that was silent but made my heart beat the loudest. A love that could only exist between a father and his son. Charles was everything I had expected of a father and more.

You are my hero, Charles.

When I gazed at Charles, Tom and my mum, I saw the meaning of everything that I experienced. I felt complete and I chose to let go of the past. All the struggle, pain and hurt. Everything I went through. I loved my two fathers more than ever before. Both of them played a major role in moulding me up to be the man I am.

I am forever indebted to you too, Tom.

My eyes shifted to mum. She was still chatting with Tasha. I loved her to the moon and back. I saw a woman who struggled and endured all the hardship for me and my brothers to acquire a decent education. It pierced me to the core. I closed my eyes and looked away.

Thank you, mum. You'll always be my guardian angel.

And finally, I glanced at Tasha, the lady who would shape my future.

"Boko!"

Mum's voice brought me out of my thoughts.

"Come here, son," she said eagerly. "I'd like to take a family photograph with Tasha."

"Move in with me Tasha," I said gazing at her over coffee. "When I am not sleeping over at your place, you're sleeping here. I have half my stuff over there and vice versa. I love waking up next to you, seeing your face. I like knowing that you'll be here at the end of a long day. And I also frigging hate cold beds."

She sat pondering over my proposition at the dining table with her breakfast. It was the weekend after graduation. Tasha had slept over at my place.

She frowned lightly. "No, you move into my place."

"My apartment is bigger. If you're worried about the bills, we can help each other. We'll discuss about it and come up with something." I stared at her anxiously as she calmly ate her breakfast.

"Okay!" She shrugged, though she was elated.

"Really?" I couldn't believe my ears.

"Of course." She laughed. "Yes, I'll move in with you."

I loved the sparkle in her eyes and her charming smile. And although we had issues, I had made up my mind. This was the lady I wanted to spend my life with.

"I love you," I said in appreciation.

Though, I had said I wouldn't rush anything, I felt like I was in a fairy tale, like everything in life was finally perfect.

I informed Charles and he seemed perfectly okay with it. He couldn't wait to meet his future daughter in-law. Tasha and I planned to spend our Christmas vacation in Lae. That was nine months away, but I couldn't wait.

EPILOGUE

Nine months later…

I glanced over to the seat on my left and saw Tasha leaning over onto my shoulder. It was an early bird flight and we checked in at three am. She was sound asleep with a smile on her face. The fringes of her hair slightly covered half of her face. I smiled at myself at the thought that she was now mine.

"You look so cute together."

Glancing over to my right, I saw an elderly couple sitting in the next row of seats. The elderly woman grinned. "Are you two going to spend your Christmas holiday in Lae?"

Her skin was wrinkled and she had white hair that fell down to her shoulders. I smiled back. "Thanks ma'am. Yeah, we're actually visiting my parents. My father especially."

"Oh, that's so sweet of you young man. I wish our sons did that George?" she said and nudged her husband.

He stirred and sat up to reveal a balding head with the little hair remaining been grey. "Yes dear," he said readjusting his glasses to look around.

I smiled at the unexpected compliment and looked back at Tasha. Will we grow old together? I thought, picturing Tasha and I as an elderly couple sitting on the porch of our own house. Yeah, we would make been old look good. I laughed quietly at the thought.

The Fokker 100 plane encountered a little turbulence and interrupted Tasha's nap. She lifted her head up sleepily and rubbed her eyes. "Hun, where are we?"

"We should be arriving at Nadzab airport soon."

Tasha peeked out of the window. "Hey Boko! Look!"

I followed her eyes, spotting a beautiful coastline and ocean. "Wow, it's beautiful."

She beamed. "I love it here already."

The plane made a sharp turn and few minutes later, the seatbelt sign came on. I fastened my seatbelt when the female flight attendant made an announcement in Tok Pisin.

"Ol man na meri, klostu nau bai yumi kamap lo Nadzab ples balus. Plis pasin sialot blo yu…"

She later translated the same announcement in English.

"Ladies and gentlemen. We're approaching the Nadzab airport. In preparation for landing, the captain has switched on the seatbelt sign. Please ensure that your seatbelt is firmly fastened and your hand luggage placed in the overhead locker…"

I glanced back at Tasha. She gave me an anxious look and I held her hand. "Relax honey, my parents will love you. I told them about you and they are really excited to meet the both of us."

My mind was filled with happiness. For the first time in my life, I didn't need to assure myself that the sun would shine tomorrow.

GLOSSARY OF TOK PISIN WORDS

Bilum	String bag
Buai	Betel nut
Bestie, buai stap ah?	My friend, do you have betelnut?
Bubu	Grandfather / Grandchild
Em stap. Wan kina lo wanpla	It's here. One kina for one
Kanaka	Native or uncivilized person
Karim leg	Courting ceremony
Kaukau	Sweet potato
Laplap	Piece of cloth or material
Meri blouse	Ladies top
Mumu	Traditional highlands style of cooking using an earth oven
Pekpek	Excreta
Pispis	Urine
Tambu	In-law
Tupla kam bestie. Kambang wantaim	Give me two, my friend. With lime too.
Wantok	Person from the same area or relative.

ABOUT THE AUTHOR

Jordan Dean was born on June 12, 1984 on Fergusson Island, Milne Bay Province, Papua New Guinea. He completed his primary and secondary education in Alotau, MBP, PNG. He has a degree in accounting and management.

He has been writing as a hobby for over a decade. He loves reading stories that gives meaning and depth to the simplest things in life. Several of his poems and short stories have been published in various magazines, anthologies and online platforms.

He is the author of '*Forbidden Dancer: A Collection of Poems*' and '*Reluctant Bride & other Short Stories from Papua New Guinea*'. He is also an observant and thoughtful essayist.